a 2:30 a.m. production

Pierdre!
Thank you very much,
It was truly a pleasure
meeting you all!
Enjoy!
M R Wright 79

Dear Jack:
Diary of an Addict

a
novel
by

Matt R. Wright

For Meagan

Table of Contents

Table of Contents

Prologue

I opened my eyes and blinked away the light film that covered my pupils every morning. The sunlight exploding through the room blinded me for a minute as my eyes adjusted to the sudden change from darkness to light. I wasn't exactly sure where I was, but the pounding in my temples led me to believe that I was having fun last night.

I sat up in a strange bed—nothing more than a futon on a metal frame only a few inches off the floor—and looked around the room. I was surrounded with white. The curtains, the walls, the carpets, the sheets, the furniture—everything was white, reflecting the early morning sun violently in every direction. The clothes that had been carelessly tossed to the floor at some point last night injected the room with an unexpected splash of color.

I rubbed my temples in a vain attempt to subside the headache that was growing worse by the second and making it hard to see anything in the too-bright colorless room. I took a deep breath, hoping that the taste of day-old beer and stale cigarettes would magically disappear with the fresh air of a new day.

I climbed out of the futon and found my boxers and pants. I pulled my phone out of my pocket. 9:45 in the morning. It felt a little weird to be out of bed before noon. I noticed my battery was less than 5%. That certainly wouldn't last much longer, and my charger did not seem to be where I was.

I put my phone down on the bed and quickly pulled on my pants while looking around for my shirt and shoes. I still had no idea whose room I was in, but I wondered where she (or he) happened to be and where she (or he) happened to keep the aspirin. I spied my gray V-neck t-shirt on the ground and threw it on. Then I grabbed my black Converse, discovered by the dresser. As I sat down on the futon to loosen the laces, the bedroom door opened.

I turned, curious to see who I would find. She was young with long brown hair, a beautiful and slightly crooked smile, and some rather obvious Jewish features. She looked at me with her huge brown eyes, and a smile crossed her face.

"You're awake," she said, standing by the door with a slight awkwardness that only accompanies the strangeness of the morning after.

"Yeah," I said. "Just woke up."

"How did you sleep?" she asked, clinging to the door as though it were a safety net, keeping her from falling into the potential danger of being in the same room with a perfect stranger.

"Good," I said, feeling the tension that rested in the space hanging between us. "Got a little headache, but other than that, I'm good."

"Leaving already?" she asked when she saw my shoes in my hand. She walked over to the bed and sat down next to me.

"I wasn't sure where you were," I said. "I thought you might have left already."

She leaned in and kissed my cheek. "You think I would let you stay in my house without me? I barely know you."

I nodded. "In all fairness, I barely know you so yes, you might have left me here alone."

She smiled and nodded slightly. I was assuming that we had met each other very late last night. Odds were, around last call. I couldn't even remember what her name was. I wasn't sure how I could tactfully go about finding out that piece of information. This wasn't the first time I had been in this situation. It probably wasn't the last time either.

"I have a toothbrush in the bathroom you can use," she said. "It's the blue one."

"You don't mind me using your toothbrush?"

"After last night," she said, "I think it's a little late to worry about germ-sharing."

I smiled, suddenly very aware of what my breath must smell like. I covered my mouth with my hand and blushed slightly.

"I should probably go and brush my teeth," I said, standing up. "By any chance do you have any aspirin, or ibuprofen, acetaminophen, or anything that might help stop this pounding in my head?"

She nodded again with her slightly crooked smile.

"Yeah," she said. "In the medicine cabinet to the left."

"Thanks," I kissed her on the forehead and walked out of the room. Cautiously I stepped down the hall, looking into each slightly open door, hoping that I didn't accidentally spy on someone who wasn't expecting me to be there. After passing a bedroom and a closet, I found the bathroom and the blue toothbrush. I quickly started to brush the funk from my mouth. While brushing, I opened the mirrored door to get the aspirin. As soon as I opened it, I stopped brushing. The toothbrush loosely hung from my mouth.

Before me were rows and rows of orange prescription bottles. I reached in and grabbed one. Adderall. I grabbed another one. Vicodin. Another one. Percocet. Another one. Lortab. Another one. Xanax.

A chill went through my body, followed by a sudden urge to grab as much as I could and get out. My heart started to race. My mouth became dry. I noticed that my hands had started to shake.

I put the toothbrush back, pulled out the aspirin bottle and quickly swallowed four of them before closing the cabinet door. I walked out of the bathroom. I stood there for a second looking down the hallway toward her bedroom and then toward the front door.

I could easily walk out the front door and forget that I had ever met this girl, whose name I couldn't remember. How bad would it really be if I left her there? Typically, I liked to say goodbye, thank you for a great time, even if I couldn't fully remember the night—or any of it, for that matter.

I also knew that if I continued to hang out with her, I might find myself in a situation that I would not be able to say no to. I had made great strides in my travels, and I didn't want to risk relapsing with a girl that I had just met because I was looking for a good time and possibly another chance to not remember sleeping with her.

I reached into my pocket for my phone, and suddenly a surge of panic took over my body. My phone was in her room. I was going to have to go back in and talk to her some more. Running was once again not an option.

I had been avoiding these situations since the day I left home. I never knew how I would do when faced with one, and luckily I had been able to make it through my first test without breaking down and grabbing as much as I could. A weaker me would have convinced myself that I was never addicted to painkillers or speed so I could happily and naively partake in all that was sitting in front of me. I felt proud that I had grown stronger since hitting the road, away from the pressures and temptations of home.

I walked back to her room and opened the door. She was lying in bed, looking up at me, still smiling.

"Your phone just rang," she said, pointing to it on the bed.

"Thanks." I walked over and picked it up, but nothing happened when I pushed the sleep button to wake it up. The battery must have died. I slid it into my pocket.

"Was it important?" she asked.

I shrugged. "Battery died. I'll find out later." I sat on the edge of the bed and picked up my shoes.

"You sure you want to leave?" she asked.

"I have a lot of stuff I need to get done," I said, not wanting to admit that I didn't trust myself around her.

"Will I see you again?" she asked.

"Of course you will," I said, knowing that I was without a doubt lying to her face. I didn't like the stigma involved with one-night stands, especially those lost in a night of an alcohol haze and blackout dreams, but I also knew that on occasion they happened.

She laughed a little. Her laugh was raspy and mildly gritty, probably the result of smoking too much at such a young age. "That didn't sound anywhere close to comforting," she said.

I looked over at her. Her brown eyes gazed at me with a level of respect that I had come to know as ill-informed adoration. I had probably told her that I was a successful writer, which I then proved by writing her a poem "on the spot" that included her name. I had used that trick many times in the past with great success, but I only attempted it when there was no way I would remember the rest of the night.

I had grown tired of the games and the lies. I really just wanted to sit down with this girl and tell her that, yes, I really wanted to see her again, to get to know her. I wanted to find a way to lie back down in bed, gingerly wrap my arm around her and fall asleep, smelling the sweet scent of her hair, as we drifted off into a dream world where everything was perfect, where life wasn't a series of disappointing endings and heartbreaking moments of clarity.

Instead, I put my shoes down, gently placed my hand against her alabaster cheek, and smiled. I leaned in and kissed her, using every ounce of passion and lust that I could muster. I pulled her close until I could feel her body pressed close to mine. We leaned back until we were lying down, wrapped in an embrace that she may have considered epic—but I was counting the moments until I knew I could slip out unnoticed.

Her breathing intensified, and I knew that she was feeling every moment of this encounter as if it were the first time she had experienced anything of the sort. I thought about how young she was and wondered if it was possible that this was the first time any man had touched this emotional level that I had worked on perfecting. Since I was never able to feel the emotions I was supposed to feel during these times, I tried to make her feel every ounce of emotion in her body. Not only with this girl but with all of them. I wanted her to cry from the enjoyment, and often times I succeeded. And while she was there, overflowing with emotion and love, I would feel something that seemed to give me life, a purpose, something that I only felt when I was using.

I didn't know how long the trail of broken hearts was, left in my wake while I searched for the pure and utter enjoyment of experiencing something other than the typical and organic feeling of breathing. Besides, this girl was young. She would be fine after a few days. Maybe one day she would even come to think of these moments fondly.

That would probably be around the same time that I would be able to lie to myself successfully.

She positioned herself on top of me, the weight of her body pressing flirtatiously against mine. I could feel her breast expand and contract with the excitement of what was about to happen. Sitting up, she pulled off the ripped t-shirt that was only slightly hanging from her body and tossed it to the side. Her perfect breasts were exposed, as much as the rest of her, to someone that wasn't even worth a glance. A slight twinge of guilt shot through my body as I carefully, softly, seductively ran my hand across her chest and up her neck, placing my hand against her cheek.

I sat up and kissed her fully. Our lips fit perfectly together, and I'm sure that in her head that meant something more than a rare and unusual coincidence. I knew the truth though, and as we slowly undressed each other, I spied around the room so that after she fell asleep in the glow of what we were about to do, I would be able to sneak out undetected. Without even a note in my place to tell her how sorry I was that I was not anywhere near the person she thought I was. I already knew she was not the person she wanted me to believe she was.

I stood in line at the coffee shop where I spent most of my days, thinking about her and wondering if she was going to be okay when she woke up. I was certain that she would be—she seemed strong. I stared up at the hand-drawn chalk menu, as if I was going to order anything different today.

When I reached the counter, I leaned down, supporting myself with my arms, smiling at the girl behind the counter.

"Hey, Neal," she said with a smile.

"Hi, Heather," I said, slightly biting my lower lip. I had often wanted to ask Heather out, but she had an intimidating quality about her that made it impossible for me to get beyond small talk and exceptionally mild flirtation. "How are you today?"

"Good," she said, shaking her head at my poor attempts at boyish charm. Any boyish charm I once had must have abandoned me years ago when I was preoccupied with losing my soul. "The usual for you?"

"Yeah," I said as I pulled my phone out of my pocket. "Would you mind if I charged this back there?" I had asked her to allow me to use her charger a few times since I had been coming in to her coffee shop.

"Of course," she said, taking my phone and plugging it in below the counter. "I hope that you didn't break her heart."

My smile faded slightly as I realized that I had become somewhat of a cliché. And if she saw me as a cliché, there were lots of other people who also saw me that way.

"She'll be fine," I said, my voice ringing with doubt.

"You know how much it is," she said with a coy smile.

I pulled $5.00 out of my pocket and smiled back. I was never able to get past that part of the conversation with Heather, and I actually preferred it that way. The air of mystery that surrounded her, along with the picture of perfection that I had built up in my head, would never be broken.

I walked over to a booth and waited for Nate, the employee working the steamer, to call my name and give me my drink. I put my bag down, then sat down myself, taking a quick moment to look around at all the people in the coffee shop.

There were stories everywhere I looked, as people walked through the door and stood in the slow moving line, as they sat at the booths, talking to friends or neighbors. The girl in the booth next to me was telling the guy she was with about her love for Jesus, and he was listening intently, pretending he actually cared. I could tell that all he wanted was to take her home that night but was too naïve to realize it wasn't going to happen. I couldn't decide which one of them was more naïve.

A few students sat adjacent to my table, discussing their biochemistry homework like quasi-experts— something about the chemical energy of metabolism. They soon switched subjects to talk about their futures as doctors. I shook my head, knowing that if they were lucky, only one of them would make it to their dream, leaving the others far behind in a fit of betrayal and heartbreak. After all, that's what friends do.

"Neal, you're up!" Nate called out from behind his wooden sanctuary that protected him from the class of people surrounding the counter, waiting like Russians in a Communist bread line for their precious coffee.

I walked up to the counter and grabbed my piping hot mocha with an extra shot of espresso. I fitted it with one of those cardboard heat-absolving sleeves to protect my hand.

"How are you today, Neal?" Nate asked, as he quickly started on the next drink in the never-ending line of them that continually grew.

"Surviving, Nate," I said, looking across the solemn faces of those standing in line. "How about you?"

"Ready for this day to be over," he said, motioning his head toward the mass of cups with orders written on them that covered his workspace.

"You'll get through it." I saluted him with my drink. "I've got to get some work done. Cheers."

"Enjoy your drink," Nate said as I walked to my table and he continued to blend together various espresso drinks.

I sat back down, took a sip of my coffee, pulled out my notebook and a pen, and started to write:

There is a world
that I have created
on sheets of paper,
and in different parts
of my ever-running mind,
where I have convinced
the person everyone sees
that this is a dream

that he will one day awake
to a world in which
he is loved and admired.
He is just asleep
and it's 1994.
A lifetime of mistakes
have all been results
of bending steel
and breaking glass.
A lifetime blinked by
with every bad decision
that has created
the person sitting beside you,
who seems a little lost
in a world
that fits him poorly,
like an ill-tailored suit.
Not that he could
ever own such things
in the sad life
he wishes to believe
is only a dream.

I put the pen down and looked over the page. Carefully, I read and reread the words, allowing each one to sink in, burrowing itself into my mind and planting a seed that desires to take root and grow. Hoping that I would be able to find something new, something worthy, something good that might find its way into the hearts and minds of people worldwide. Deep down I knew that if I was lucky it would reach even one other person, and make him think, if only for a minute.

"Mind if I sit?" a voice said as I reread what I had written for the fifth time.

I looked up to see Heather standing table-side, wearing skin tight black jeans and matching shirt that showed every curve of her body in a flattering way. Her smile sat playfully on her face, and her hazel eyes danced in her head. In her hand was a plate of organic corn chips and freshly made, organic salsa. Must be break time.

"Please," I said, grabbing my bag from the chair so she could sit.

She put her plate down and sat. I gave her an awkward smile, unsure of what to say. She had breached the protective barrier that I had strategically kept between us, creating an entirely new dynamic to the non-relationship that we shared. This was no longer about mutual niceties and politeness, now it would have to be based on honest-to-goodness respect and a series of potentially shared interests. I wasn't sure how to react to her brazen move.

"What are you working on?" she asked, as she dipped a chip into her salsa and took a small bite, being extra careful not to spill over herself.

"Nothing really," I said. "Just a poem."

"Can I read it?"

She looked at me as she carefully licked a touch of salsa from the corner of her mouth. I looked down at the poem, and then back at her. I did want other people to enjoy my work. Slowly I slid my notebook across the table.

I watched as her eyes moved back and forth across each line, occasionally jumping back to reread something, presumably to make a decision on how she interpreted each line, every word, the poem as a whole.

There was something voyeuristic about watching someone read my work. I equated it to videotaping myself in the act of making love and then watching it later to experience the entire manifestation of joy all over again. The ability to watch something I've created cause happiness, sorrow, or simply an opportunity for someone to think about her life and what it all means—if any of it means anything at all—is a joy that is better than self-gratification. Unlike self-gratification, it can only be practiced with another person present.

"Wow," she said, as she finished reading. "So...you think this life is nothing more than a dream?"

"I wish parts of it were only a dream," I said, looking away slightly. "Did you like it?"

"It's good," she said, taking a bite of another chip. "What parts do you wish were dreams?"

I smiled and bit my lip slightly. "The past."

"All of it?"

"Most of it," I said. "Enough to reset me."

She cocked her head slightly to the side and looked at me with concern in her eyes. "You're a nice guy, Neal. Everyone here likes you. You are obviously talented. Everything from your past made you who you are. Why would you want to reset yourself?"

"I think that it is slightly arrogant to say you couldn't be a better person than who you are now," I explained.

"Maybe I would be completely different than who I am today if I changed or erased parts of my past, but who's to say that I wouldn't be better?"

She took another bite of her chips and looked at me as she thought about her next response. I smiled slightly. It had been a long time since I had talked philosophy with anyone, not since I left so long ago.

The past year and a half seemed to have gone by in the blink of an eye, but at the same time, it felt like I left a lifetime ago. This was exactly how I would have spent a Tuesday morning with my friends in Virginia—nursing a hangover, writing, and discussing different philosophies of life. I missed them a little more than usual at the moment.

"Couldn't you just as easily say that you may have become a worse person than who are?" she asked, arrogantly grinning.

"Valid point," I said. "It truly is nothing more than speculation...and hope...that you would have done things correctly if you could go back and redo them."

"So the arrogant view is that you couldn't be a better person, not that you would do things better the second time around?"

I couldn't really argue. Both were rather arrogant viewpoints. I guess the answer mainly depended on whether or not you wanted a chance to change your past for the hopes of a better present. Entirely individual.

"I suppose," I said. "It just depends on if you want to change things about your past or not."

She smiled wider and held a chip in her hand, waving it over me in a display of victory.

"And what do you think would make you a better person?" she asked. "What would you so readily change about your past?"

And there it was. I hated that question more than I hated any question in the history of the world. In a lifetime filled with mistakes, how could I pick out the one mistake that quite possibly changed my life forever? I had it pinpointed to one moment, one individual instance. There never has been an answer more perfect for any question in the history of the world, and I never wanted to give it to anyone.

"Tell me, Neal," she said, as she dipped her chip. "What would you change about your past?"

The smile quickly faded from my face. No one outside of a very small group of people knew who I really was, and I had done everything within my power to keep from showing the real me to anyone else.

I looked into Heather's hazel eyes and sighed as memories flooded back to me. Twice today I was reminded of a past life that I wanted nothing more than to forget.

"Dying," I said. My gaze remained unwavering as I let her process my one-word answer. It was the only explanation I was willing to give.

Her eyes filled with confusion, concern, and sadness all at once.

"Do you mean that you wish you had died?" she asked.

I shook my head and looked away. The pain of the memory flooded my entire body.

"I'll be right back," I said as I stood and walked to the bathroom. I closed the door behind me and slid the latch, locking myself in. Resting my head against the white paneling, I closed my eyes. My hands had started to shake a little when I was sitting at the table with Heather, but they had since moved on to full fledged convulsions.

I turned around and slid my back against the door until I was seated on the floor, my head between my knees. My head suddenly felt like it was filled with pressure, and a ringing that had been planted in my ears kept getting louder, to the point where I couldn't hear anything else. The ringing screamed, deafening me. I covered my ears in hopes of subduing the siren-like sounds, but it was no help.

My hands shook terribly, and I felt my eyes welling up with tears behind my closed lids. I clinched them tighter, wishing that the ordeal would come to a quick end. Sweat started to drip from my forehead, sliding down my face and falling to the ground.

My body was tense, and my joints started to ache. I wanted to stretch them out, but it hurt to move any muscle in my body. I begged for the pain to end. I wanted to feel normal. I wanted to be normal. I wished that every decision I had made leading up to this moment was non-existent. I didn't want to be me anymore. I wanted to be someone completely different. I wanted to be someone that didn't have to deal with the constant struggle I had literally injected myself with.

I hated myself. I hated who I had become. I hated my life and what little I stood for. In an evaporating haze of broken dreams and promises I had made to myself—and others—I felt my life slowly ending. I wished that I could simply take myself out of the world to make room for someone else who would be able to make a difference. A life of wasted dreams resulted in nothing more than a wasted life.

I felt the door push slightly against my back, snapping me out of my past-induced trance. Another coffee-filled customer must need to use the facility. I ached from head to toe. Sweat covered my face, and I could feel that it had soaked into my shirt. My hands were still trembling, and I was slightly afraid that my legs weren't going to work when I finally stood up again.

I wiped the tears from my eyes, and reaching up to the sink, I pulled myself to standing. I placed all of my weight on the porcelain bowl and hoped that it was firmly attached to the wall.

From within the large mirror, my reflection stared at me—red face, bloodshot and puffy eyes. The tears had stained tiny saltwater pathways on my face that cracked when I moved my mouth or blinked. I turned the water on and waited for the steam to rise.

I leaned down and used my cupped hands to splash the extraordinarily hot water against my face. I wished that the hot water could melt away every memory of the person I kept running from, but knew he would always be deep inside. I knew that I would cling to that person in an attempt to hold on to a dream that I used to believe in. Letting go of someone that you used to be is not as easy as people say it should be. Saying goodbye to an old friend is very difficult; saying goodbye to yourself is nearly impossible.

I wiped the excess water from my face and exited the bathroom where the young hipster with Buddy Holly glasses, a bad mustache, and extremely tight jeans was waiting with a very impatient look on his face. He kind of scowled at me as he shoved past me into the bathroom, closing the door and violently locking it.

I walked back toward the table where Heather was still sitting. She looked up at me as I approached.

"Neal," she said, her voice filled with concern and a mild amount of fear. "You don't look so good."

"Yeah," I said. I nodded. "I'm not feeling so good."

Heather quickly stood and pulled out my seat for me. "Here," she said. "Sit down. I'll go get you some water."

I sat down, and held my head in my hands. The façade that I could normally put on had been stripped away from me during my time in the bathroom, battling the demons that plague me day in and day out. Anything that may have attracted Heather to me moments before I walked into the bathroom had surely disappeared in the time that I was gone. My past was a cross that I had to carry. I knew that not everyone could accept a past such as the one that I had procured for myself. I had come to acknowledge these truths. In another life, I knew I would have problems dealing with someone who had been through the same things I had.

Heather came back with some water and my phone. "Here," she said, handing me the glass of water and putting the phone on the table. "Drink this."

I took a sip of water. It was the first hydrating liquid I had drunk in days. After that one single sip I felt slightly more whole than I had only moments before. I took a deep breath and shook my head. I felt embarrassed. I couldn't believe that in the first real conversation I had with this woman, I regressed to the person I had pushed so deep down inside I thought he would never again see the light of day.

"Feel better?" she asked, after I finished off half the glass.

I nodded and looked at her. She radiated beauty. There was a purity about her that was absolutely magnetic. There was a sweetness to her that could only be authentic. Nobody could fake the niceties that she exuded. I thought that maybe I was so attracted to her because she was the exact opposite of who I was on the inside.

She sat back down across from me, reached out, and placed her soft hand on top of mine. "What was that?" she asked.

I looked down at her hand, and I could tell that she truly cared about what I was going through. "I don't know," I said. "I just think I'm not exactly feeling like myself today."

She smiled. "We all have days like that," she said, lightly stroking my hand.

I smiled back at her, and the feelings of fear and regret that had been resonating throughout my body slowly started to subside, replaced by something else. Something new. It was a strange sensation. I looked into her hazel eyes, and suddenly I started to wonder if this new sensation was admiration of some sort. I started to wonder if all the playful small talk and adolescent flirting had actually grown into a form of respect. Did I actually have feelings for this woman?

"I have to get back to work," she said, patting my hand lightly with hers. "Glad you feel better."

"Thanks," I said, forcing a smile. I felt awkward and out of place in my own body for the first time since I had beat the addictions and started to see the world clearly again.

Heather looked back at me as she walked behind the counter and went back to work.

I had never wanted to get rid of the fear and the anger inside of me more than I did at that moment. I didn't want to have to worry about having a breakdown while talking with someone. Somehow I fumbled my way through it this time, but I didn't know how I would respond if it happened again. I knew that I was going to have to face this buried part of me soon. I knew it would have to be exorcised. I thought I would be able to hide it forever, but apparently it didn't want to remain hidden.

Glancing around the coffee shop, I wondered if anyone else was dealing with the same torment that I was going through. The memories of my wasted past, talents, and abilities hung before me as a constant reminder of the person I could have been if I had just been a little smarter, a little stronger. I wished, more than ever before, for the integrity that my parents had tried to instill in me.

When I turned my phone back on, I heard the voicemail chime. As I waited for the voicemail prompts to pass, I watched Heather taking orders. By smiling and being genuinely happy, she brought a few moments of joy to whomever she was talking to. I wondered if she was one of those people who were actually happy, those people that I envied on occasion. There were times I wanted to be one of those people. They would take risks and chances in areas of life that I never would because they believed in and trusted people. I stopped trusting when I became someone not worth trusting.

I knew that Heather and I were never meant to be. I was not the type of person someone like Heather could ever want. I was a bad person, not worthy of someone that could so easily bring joy into the lives of others.

I hit play on the voicemail, smiling at the thought of a night of solace with her and enveloping myself in the idea of a life I knew I was not born to live.

Suddenly, everything changed.

The voice on the other end of the phone was one from my past. I hadn't spoken to Rich in six months, and even then it was barely a conversation. He was in pain, and he had asked for a favor, just one tiny little favor.

I could feel the color in my face fade away. I went from being red and puffy to pale and frail. Heather looked over at me and must have seen a serious change in my appearance because she immediately ran over to check on me.

"Neal," she said. "Are you okay?"

"Yeah," I said, nodding my head as I put my phone down. "I just, I have to go."

She looked at me, bewildered. "Go?" she asked. "Where are you going?"

"Virginia," I said, quickly packing up, shoving everything that was sitting in front of me into my backpack.

"Virginia?" she asked again.

I nodded as I tossed my backpack over my shoulder and stood up.

"What's in Virginia?" she asked.

I looked at her, and wasn't really quite sure what to say. I never considered it my home, and I hardly had any connections left there.

"What's in Virginia?" she asked again.

I shrugged. A momentary thought about kissing her passionately flitted through my mind. I shook it off and said the only thing that could define Virginia to me. "My past." I shook my head and raised my arms helplessly. "I'm sorry," I said, slowly backing away from Heather and walking down the few stairs that separated the two floors of the coffee shop. "I have to go."

I turned and ran out the door, throwing my bag into my car as I jumped into the front seat. New life had been suddenly injected into me. I was excited about a new adventure. I was going back to Virginia, and with that meant seeing my old friends, coming face to face with my old life, and possibly meeting a new beginning.

I turned the engine. As I pulled out of the parking spot I thought about my experiences here and how they would add to the many that continually shaped the person I had and would become.

Heading for 40 East, I wondered if I ever would get to a point where all of my experiences, including all of the mistakes I had made and had spent so long running from, would finally get me to a point where I could forgive myself for the things I had done.

I.

I walked into Rich's room. It was dark. The tiny space was cluttered with piles of clothing and garbage. A stale odor stung my nose, a pungent mixture of sweat, piss and shit that could only come from weeks of not showering and using anywhere but the toilet as a bathroom. It took my eyes a second to adjust to the dim light. I scanned the room, looking for an inhabitant.

"Rich?" I called, pulling out a cigarette and lighting it. The sweet scent of the cigarette smoke was a welcome change to the stench that was currently burning my nostrils. "Where you at, kid?"

From the darkness of the room, Rich's meager voice called out softly, "Neal, please don't smoke in here." It surprised me, his voice. Its weakness the complete opposite from his once confident and commanding assertions.

I turned to find him squatting in the far corner, the darkest area of the room. His head hung, facing the ground, his arms straight down with his wrists touching as though he was cuffed to the floor. He remained perfectly still, statuesque in a creepy sort of way that made a chill shoot through my body. I had to physically shake it off. Taking a drag of my cigarette, I quietly watched him. Even though I had just heard him speak, I wondered how a person who was so obviously dead could be squatting like that.

"Why not?"

"I don't like the way it smells," he said.

I walked over to him and smiled. "I think this cigarette is the least of your worries right now."

I sat down next to him. The odor emanating from his body was almost unbearable. I noticed that he had dyed and cut his hair. The last time I saw him it was light brown and long enough to tuck behind his ears; now it was short and black, spiked up erratically, surprisingly trendy. Rich despised trendy. His face was sheet white and hollowed out. He couldn't have weighed more than 120 pounds. Used to seeing a tanned, 165-pound man, the site of him set me aback. I was not prepared to see him in this condition.

"You look like shit, man."

"Amazingly enough that means I look better than I feel."

A quiet belch left his mouth, followed by a small amount of bile that fell to the floor, adding to a pile that appeared to have been collecting for quite some time. Rich's body didn't even flinch. He had become so accustomed to throwing up that the act didn't even faze him anymore. I could see from the small pile of vomit in front of him that he had started throwing up blood—a sure sign that his stomach hadn't seen any nourishment for God knows how long.

"You on anything?" I asked. I knew about Rich's problems. I assumed that's why he asked me to come. He had bottomed out a long time ago, and I figured he was finally realizing it.

"No, you got anything?" He looked up at me. His eyes were gray and yellow. They appeared lifeless and empty yet filled with hope at the idea that I might have something to ease his immediate pain.

I ignored his plea, tossing it to the side as a poor attempt at humor, but fearing that he was serious and in desperate need of something that would bring him back to feeling normal, his version of normal.

"When was the last time you used?" I asked.

"Yesterday," he said.

This would explain why he was sitting on the floor in a pile of his own piss and vomit. The first day was unbelievably painful, emotionally, physically, and mentally. The amount of will power that it takes to make it through that day alone is something that very few possess. Looking at Rich now, I knew he could crack at any moment.

"When was the last time you ate?" I asked, fearing this answer almost as much as the previous one.

"Thursday...I think." He sounded even weaker as the words left his mouth as if he suddenly realized the reality of his self-imposed condition. It was now Tuesday.

"Come on, get up," I said as I stood and offered him my hand.

"Where are we going?"

"You are getting in the shower, then I'm going to buy you something to eat."

"I don't want to eat."

"I don't care," I said. "We have to get you out of this house."

"I'm not fucking hungry, Neal," he bellowed at me. The joyous side effects of drug withdrawal include sudden bursts of anger, usually directed at someone who is not the cause of the anger.

"Feel better?" I asked. "Now that you got that out of your system."

He looked up at me with his yellow and grays with anger and disdain. I smiled back down at him and offered my hand once again. He took it, and I helped him to his feet. He stumbled a little as he stood but regained his balance by placing his hand on my shoulder.

A cloud of stink rose from the ground. I could see a green and brown stain on the carpet. Rich clearly hadn't moved since he last used yesterday. I doubted if he had showered in days. The strong mixture of vomit, urine, and shit hit my nose, and I had to hold back from throwing up.

"Where've you been for the past few months, Rich?"

"Here," he said. "Inside these walls. Where have you been?"

"Everywhere but here," I said, looking around the room, back at the life I had before I decided it was time to leave.

Rich walked into the bathroom and knelt over the toilet. More chunks of his stomach came up in a mixture of green and red phlegm. He coughed up the last of it, wiped his mouth and then sat on the side of the tub to start the shower.

He took off his shirt and flung it into a pile of laundry that appeared to have been collecting for months. His chest was barren, with a slightly yellowish hue to it. I could easily count his bones.

"Why did you call me now, after all this time?" I asked, averting my eyes for a quick second. I almost felt like I was looking at something I wasn't supposed to, and the feeling of being ashamed washed over my body. The site of Rich in this condition made me revert to a little child in my mind. It was the same feeling I got when I first realized my parents weren't immortal.

He turned to look at me. Tears were streaming down his face, but not because he was sad, or because he was hurting. He cried because his body needed him to cry. He needed to release all the badness and filth that had been stored inside for so long.

"Because I need you here, Neal," he said, wiping at his eyes as more tears continued to fall. "You were here when I started this journey, and you have to be here now. When I finish it."

"Don't worry. I'm here for you." I knew it was a cookie cutter reassurance, but I didn't know what else to say.

"And the others, they need to be here too," he said, sticking his hand into the shower to test the temperature.

I paused. The thought of all of us together again made me cringe.

"I can get Chris here."

"I can get Johnson here." He turned and shut the door.

I stared blankly at the closed door. I promised Rich Chris, but I didn't know if I could deliver. He promised me

Johnson, and I hoped he couldn't deliver. The last time I had spoken to Rich was six months ago. I hadn't seen him in two years, not since I left Virginia. He was an addict then, but over those two years he slid down the scale of addiction to full-blown junkie. Part of me definitely felt guilty. I introduced him to so much.

I had kept in contact with Chris. He had also gone straight. He quit writing, had a real job now. His dreams of driving around the country and being a writer disappeared as he grew older, and disappointment and rejection made him callous about submitting his work.

And Johnson, I hadn't talked to him in three years. Not since Kate. She was the girl from Trenton. A girl. How prosaic. We always said we would be brothers forever. I guess that was until a girl came between us. I had no idea who he was anymore, what his life looked like. Would we get along? We had to be there for Rich. We had to let go of our past grievances, at least for the moment.

As Rich showered I picked up the notebook he had on the end table and began to flip through the pages until I reached the final entry. It was dated five months prior. There was a time when Rich couldn't go five days without writing something new, much less five months. It was a poem entitled, "For Claire, Where Ever I May Find You."

Last night I awoke,
but I was still dreaming.
You were standing on a rain-drenched street,
your hair was wet,
you were waiting for me.
I stood and stared,

as the rain fell on my head.
You smiled at me,
beckoned for me to come closer
the harder I ran
the further away you were.
I wanted to catch you
hold you in my arms
feel your breath
touch my skin.
The harder I run,
the more I love you.
You never understood
how happy I could make you.
How I never want to wake up
from the dream which you inspired.
When we meet,
I stare into your eyes,
I reach out to you
and I hold your hand.
I HOLD YOUR HAND!
Thank you for loving me tonight.
I'm sorry I have to wake up now,
hopefully you'll be here tomorrow.

I stepped outside on the patio to call Chris. Chris Franklyn was the type of guy that was slightly ashamed of his preferences in life, living in a continual state of fear and worry about his decisions. He constantly thought that he would regret doing something, or not doing something so he always ended up regretting, no matter what he decided. Every girl, every move, every story he submitted that was rejected, and every story that he never turned in. He regretted all of it. He second-guessed and rethought every decision he had ever made, but he hid it behind a façade of arrogance and smiles.

After two rings he answered.

"Chris, it's Neal."

"Holy shit! How the fuck are you?"

"Alive, brother. You?"

"Progressing," he said.

"Good for you."

"What have you been doing with your self?"

I could hear the telltale metallic ting of a Zippo being flicked open and the igniter being scraped across the flint before he inhaled deeply.

"Unimportant right now."

"Why, what's up?" He sounded concerned.

I had to give it to Chris. That man was loyal. He had been there for me so many times in the past. He knew secret upon secret of mine and always kept them locked in his vault of a mind.

"Nothing with me. Rich needs us," I said.

"Fuck Rich," he said. The words cut through the phone like a samurai's sword. I never expected Chris to say words like that about Rich. The two of them were the closest of our group. You rarely heard Chris's name without Rich's following it shortly after.

"What? What do you have against Rich?"

"My life doesn't need to be dictated by some cracked out junkie."

Suddenly I was angry. It took a lot to get me there, but hypocrites did it to me every time. Chris was the one who first started using, and he had fallen more times than any of us. Every time he started using again, it was worse than the time before. And every time he quit, he became more judgmental about anyone who used.

"He's always been there for you. He has seen you through many hard times," I said quietly. I could feel my face growing red as I tried to stay calm.

"Rich told me I strayed, that I sold out, that I was no longer one of you all," he said. I could hear the hurt in his voice. "He said that I never really believed in us or in myself. So fuck him. I don't need to be associated with him."

I would never say it to Chris, but Rich was right. Chris never did believe in his own talent, much less anyone else's.

"Chris, don't be a self-righteous asshole," I said through clinched teeth. "You brought us together, you created this group, and you can't turn your back on us, even if you want to. You're just too loyal of a person."

"What does he need? Money?" Sarcasm dripped off his words.

"He's quitting," I said.

"Oh, please." His voice rang with the same ignorant tone that people have when they say criminals can't be reformed. "Neal, he's a fucking junkie."

"Chris, you were a junkie. Don't you remember the morning I came home and you were searching the carpet fibers for just the smallest crack rock?" I asked. "You weren't even smoking crack at the house! I was a junkie. I shot more shit into my veins…"

I paused. Every time I thought about those days, a chill shot through my body, my stomach twisted in pain, and I suddenly felt like I needed to use again.

"He needs us," I continued. "You turn your back now, the story ends, and it's over. He's done, we're done, and what kind of ending would that be?"

Chris was silent. I could hear his mind racing.

"Chris, we all strayed from the path of success that we dreamed we would pave. You did, I did, and Rich did."

"What about Johnson?" The mockery that hung from those words sent me reeling in anger. I wanted to tell Chris to fuck off and throw my phone off the balcony, but I held it in.

"You know he did," I said, biting my tongue. "And even he's coming back."

"Is Kate coming with him?"

The dagger stung. It took my breath away, made it impossible to talk. I stood there in utter amazement at the asshole on the other end of the line, wondering how and why this guy was my closest friend.

"I'm sorry, Neal. That was low."

Oxygen filled my lungs. I was flustered but knew how to counter. Chris never worked well with guilt so I played those cards.

"Rich wants to feel again. Do you remember what it was like to not feel...anything? He wants to feel something, he wants to be able to love, he wants to stop hating himself. If you remember what any of that was like, meet us at the diner at 1:00. If not, fuck off, okay?"

I hung up the phone and squeezed the banister with all my might. The cool winter air whipped around my body, and I was reminded of pulling Chris away from the cliff's edge so long ago. It was a chilly winter night, just like this one, and he looked exactly like Rich, emaciated and tormented. He was strung out from a many weeks long cocaine and crack binge that had all but destroyed his once strong and caring soul.

He hated everyone and everything, especially himself. Convinced that he wouldn't be able to quit and lost in a battle of self-loathing that buried itself deeper in the back of his mind than anyone could imagine, he stood at the edge of a cliff and told me it was time to abandon it all. It was time for him to stop the madness, the questions, the constant battles that he had with himself, and the bevy of voices he constantly heard in his head. This was going to be his poetic ending to the life that he had successfully ruined, his final feeble attempt at being an artist.

I told him he was crazy, that he didn't realize the repercussions of jumping. I tried to explain to him that so many people needed him, that he didn't realize how much he was loved. He turned to look at me and said, "The fire, the brimstone, the eternity of pain, if there is a hell, or another stretch on this planet as another human in another life, could not be any worse than where I am every day."

Then he jumped. I never was quite sure how I stopped him, but I did. I handled everything for him after that, for a while. He couldn't function. He was lost in a sea of confusion and self-contempt, dealing with a sadness that came from wanting to die but unable to succeed. Months passed and slowly he came back around. Once he was able to function alone, I left to let him live his life. I knew he remembered this, and I knew he would be at the diner tonight.

Diary Entry I:

Dear Jack,

Chris's been bringing this girl around recently. She seems to be nice enough, not the sharpest tool in the shed, but really, can he expect much more? I don't really like her, but how can I tell my brother that his girl rubs me more raw than sandpaper. She is also a massive pothead, and we both know how Chris is. He will start using, just to stay close to her, and he'll bring it around us, and well, it'll all go down hill from there. I don't want to travel down that road though.

Anyway, they are all bridges, some we cross, some we avoid, some we fucking torch. I guess I'll find out what I do to this one when I get to it, if I get to it. Chris wouldn't steer us wrong. We have a path, and we are following it strictly.

I should go. Feeling sorry and down today. Must hold lively and verbal conversation with someone who can reply.

From one subterranean to another,

Rich Stevens

II.

Rich didn't say a word for an hour after his shower. After getting dressed, he sat around for a while, staring at everything and nothing at the same time. He was in another world, a world that he didn't want anyone else to be a part of. Every so often his entire body would convulse, and he would run to the bathroom to throw up or purge himself of some other form of disgusting that was festering inside of him.

I sat by, off to the side, waiting for him to speak. I spent dark, lonely hour remembering things from the past. How the four of us met, the trips we took together, the times we spent in silence with pens in hand. We used to gather in a room, pens feverishly working, spitting out words and sayings that we hoped would go down in the annals of time as some of the greatest things ever said, when suddenly one of us would stop and shout out, "I took to following my heart but got lost when it stopped beating," or some other writing that struck us as particularly brilliant.

We would get lost in an empty canvas of lined paper. Like great artists throwing paint, we spewed ink. It dripped from the points of our pens and created a collective brilliance that could be seen when all of our work was put side by side. Almost everything we wrote was depressing, yet upbeat, with just a glimmer of hope shining somewhere in the background. We were all in need of something that was missing, in search of the ultimate dream of contentment and happiness. Our lives were built on dreams, dreams that we were never able to achieve.

"She didn't even recognize me," Rich said monotonously, breaking the silence.

"Who?" I asked, rather confused by the only statement he had made since his shower.

"Never mind."

I pulled my watch out of my pocket and realized that it was almost one. If Chris was going to be at the diner, he would be there soon. I glanced up at Rich, but he had gone back to his world.

"Come on, Rich, let's go."

He nodded and slowly stood. He looked so weak. I wanted to help, but I knew that was not something his ego could handle. He looked at me.

"What's up?" I asked.

"Grab that tape recorder on the table." He pointed to a voice recorder across the room.

"What for?"

"A Knight," he said in a way that sounded like I was the stupid one.

"What are you talking about?"

"Get me the fucking recorder!" he shouted, rubbing his temples, the withdrawal anger shining through again. "Before I forget."

I handed him the tape recorder, and with a shaky hand, he hit record.

"I sit and stare at the apparitions of a memory that I had almost forgotten. Life spins off its axis and shades itself from the sun, hiding from the truth, cloaked in distrust. I awaken to dreams and sleep to reality. I feel a knight that slayed the dragon. But the princess turned her back to unveil her disgust for masculine games. The conquest of a weak man, make the little people proud, the one that matters turns away. I imagine my bed, once again, prepared for the eternal rest. I've accomplished nothing, but see nothing left to dream for. A division of pride departed the distraction that only love can bring."

He hit the stop button and tossed it back to me.

"Can you write that down for me sometime?" he asked.

"Yeah, no problem," I said, still in awe from the powerful performance he gave in his delivery. "Why do you need me to?"

"I can't write anymore," he said as he grabbed his jacket and walked out the door and down the stairs with me following closely behind.

We got into the car and headed to the diner. Rich stared out the window, noticing the houses, the cars, the businesses as if he was seeing them for the first time, even though he had seen them every day for years.

"Do you know how long it has been since I have actually seen all of this?" he asked.

"No idea. How long?"

"I don't know. I'm not sure if I'm even seeing them now." Rich turned and stared back out the window. "Did you call Chris?"

"Yeah, I think he'll be here."

"He still mad at me?"

"Who can really tell with Chris?"

Rich let out an inaudible mutter and leaned his head back against the headrest and closed his eyes. "Johnson will be there."

I had been hoping that Rich hadn't called Johnson. I didn't want to see him any more than Chris wanted to see Rich. As far as the terminations of friendships could go, our fallout had been epic. Bridges were crossed that friends should never cross unless it's final. As they say, some things can't be taken back.

"Great, it'll be good to have the four of us together again," I said through clenched teeth.

"You lie worse than I did to my probation officer."

"You've never been arrested," I countered.

He shrugged as he looked out the window. "I should have been," he said, sounding like he almost wished that he had been.

I looked over at him, and I could see on his face that he was slowly waiting for time to become a tangible thing again.

We pulled into the parking lot. Through the front window I could see Chris and Johnson already sitting in our old booth, drinking coffee, and smoking cigarettes. It took me back to a time when life seemed easier, like there was a real possibility of happiness. Tonight though, life didn't feel happy. Tonight felt ominous. A shadow of gloom blanketed the air.

Rich got out of the car and headed for the diner. I sat still, staring at the scene in the window. Life happened all around the world; we made life happen while sitting at that booth.

Rich turned and looked back at me. "Are you coming?"

I reached into the backseat and grabbed my notebook. before getting out of the car. "Come on." I smiled. "Let's get you something to eat."

Diary Entry II:

Dear Jack,

    Chris and I headed out the other day and got high. It was the first time I actually felt the effects of what Chris so endearingly refers to as the 'King Green.' And I must say, WOW. Everything was magnified—my hearing, my sight, my taste, all of my sensations. I can see why people like to do it all the time. In my haze I placed my pen against a piece of paper, and out of the ink cartridge spilled this little opus that Neal, Chris, and Johnson have sung high praises about. I find it to be choppy and incoherent. Tell me what you think.

    Justice comes,
    And then it goes.
    I close my eyes,
    I am in a place
    Where the bee
    Rests on the bone
    That has no marrow.
    The rope is loose
    Along the ground
    Going nowhere,
    Leading to the silver shackle.
    The stagnant water

Looks inviting
But is cold.
The weeds are long
The garden is dead
The hero stuck
In the net
Hanging from
The tree.
The villain laughs
And scurries away,
Running from
The pain he sees.
Justice came,
And then it went.
The frog is a stone
That cannot move.
The acorn
Cannot sprout.
The clouds
Refuse to change
And the clock
Is stuck
Where the bee
Rests on the bone
That has no marrow.

Let me know, my brother. I must head out. Chris and I are going to Michelle's.

From one subterranean to another,
Rich Stevens

III.

As I walked into the diner I could feel the eyes of all the old regulars turn to stare at Rich and me. It had been years since I had been there, and I was willing to bet that Rich couldn't remember the last time he was there either. I was amazed at the fact that I still knew the majority of people sitting there. Time seemed to change all things, except for the people who have nothing to do at 1:00 in the morning in the middle of the week.

We made our way to the table, and Miss Claudia came over to say hi.

"Hi, boys. I have not seen you for a long time," she said, her thick accent dripping like honey into our ears. Miss Claudia was a Jamaican refugee who came to the United States with her family after a hurricane destroyed their home. She was 16 then, and after leaving school at 17, she started working at the diner. Thirty years later, she was still there, and she remembered the names of every regular that she ever had.

"Hi, Miss Claudia. How've you been?" I asked.

"Good, Neal. I've missed you boys." She turned to look at Rich. "How's life, Rich?"

He forced a smile and choked out the words, "In progress."

"That is good…I think," she said, a confused look crossing her face. "Well, Chris and Johnson are at your usual table. Two coffees, I assume?"

"Please," I said as we continued to the table. Rich looked like he was in more pain with each passing step. I started to question if he was ready for what I was putting him through. I didn't want to push him too hard too fast. He was at a fragile point in the process, not to mention in his life.

Johnson and Chris were looking over at us. I could feel a knot growing in my stomach with the anticipation. Tension was unavoidable. I hoped we would look past it, at least for tonight.

I took a seat next to Chris, and Rich slid in next to Johnson. Chris hadn't changed at all. He still had the same haircut and same baby face. He never could grow any facial hair. He was even sporting the same style—a white button-down and Khaki pants. Johnson had changed since the last time I saw him, but it had also been three years. His hair was longer, thick and wild, and he had grown a "chin-strap" goatee. His naturally tanned skin had faded a little, giving him a more mysterious appearance. He was wearing baggy pants and a shirt that was about two sizes too big for him. He looked like any coffee shop misanthrope from the mid-nineties.

The tension was thick. It was clear that we all felt strange sitting together at our table again. Rich felt it more than the rest of us.

"Thank you guys for being here. I appreciate it," he said, breaking the silence.

"Rich," Chris started. He seemed nervous to be with us again. Face to face, Chris lost a lot of the confidence he had on the phone. "I hope this goes well for you. I wish you the best of luck, and I am here for you through it...and I'm sorry that I've been such a huge dick over the past year."

He stopped talking and looked down to the table before taking a strained sip of coffee. Johnson looked at me, and I glanced at him. I suddenly felt a twinge of regret for allowing our friendship to fall by the wayside, but I still didn't want to speak with him.

Miss Claudia came over and smiled down at us. "Boys, it is so good to see you all again. It is like a reunion with all four Beatles."

"I imagine that would be difficult," Johnson said with a grin.

"Oh, but it is just good to see you all together again," she said, her smile standing out prominently on her perfectly black skin. "I imagine you all want the usual."

In unison we all nodded as we handed her our unopened menus.

"Four steak and cheese with extra mayo. I'll be right back with those." Miss Claudia walked away, and again we sat in silence.

All of the anger, all of the mistrust, everything hung in the air. Everything that had taken our once unbreakable group and broken it down to meager connections and random, pithy phone calls. Every memory of every fight, every proverbial knife that had been stuck in a friend's back was lying in front of us. Our eyes shifted toward each other, then away again. It felt as though we had all just broken up and were sitting in that awkward moment before one of us inevitably stormed out causing a scene embarrassing everyone else at the table.

"Damn it, guys!" Rich screamed, after what seemed like an eternity of silence. "Talk. Talk about anything. I need you all to be the way that you were, for me to be me again. Argue, debate, talk about philosophy. Just fucking talk."

We all stared at each other, waiting, hoping for someone to say something that could spark conversation.

"So Neal, how's the writing going?" Johnson asked with a slight hesitation in his words. He pointed to my notebook.

I could see that even speaking to me broke his soul a little bit. He didn't want to ask me that question, and I certainly didn't want to respond. I thought about Kate and everything that had happened, then quickly shook it off.

"It's alright, I guess, nothing worth bragging about, but I have a few things I really like." I lied. I had no reason to lie, but I did. There was a lot in my notebook that I liked. I guess I was trying to downplay it a bit for their sake. They had no idea what had been going on with my career since I had left.

"Read us something," Chris said, trying his hardest to keep the conversation going.

"Alright." I searched through my book looking for something to read. "Oh, alright, I wrote this up in New York, a few years ago. Actually, I was driving out of New York when I wrote it. Honestly, I don't remember what I was thinking about at the time, but it's probably my favorite recent piece of work. It's called 'Service Boy.'"

I cleared my throat and scanned the page quickly.

"I never had to tell anyone
what I thought
or how I felt.
No one ever asked,
no one ever cared.
I always agreed with them
and delivered lip-sync love.
Now I'm stuck in limbo,
trying to solve the enigmatic.
The fatuous thoughts
of a confused little boy
trample the sanity
of a stable man.
I am lost in an area
of confusion and lust,
a zone of bitterness and love.
And all I ask is,
'Can you fix me?'
I used to scoff at that,
deny that anything was wrong,
and contend that I was okay.
Now I can see,
and it's a sight that liquefied
my stony heart.
I'm just a child
with so much to learn.
I'm searching for a teacher

that knows about fear
and can tell me about love and lust.
Explain the thoughts
that plague my afflicted mind.
None of it matters though.
Tell me I'm wrong.
Feelings are only weapons
used by others to achieve
their selfish goals.
I'm nothing but a pawn
in everybody's game,
not even the king of my own.
Use me, abuse me,
I am at your service.
Here to do your bidding.
When you are done with me,
pass me off to someone else
and forget about the one,
the only one who was honest,
who bared his innocence
and lost himself in you."

I took a deep breath and looked up from my notebook. Rich, Johnson, and Chris stared at me. Their faces were blank and vacant. I kept waiting for one of them to say something, but they all just stared, lifeless.

"Damn, was it that bad?" I asked. I had only read that one to a few people in the past, and they had all said they loved it. I suddenly wondered if I had inadvertently surrounded myself with people who would tell me they liked anything I wrote, the sycophants, instead of giving me an honest opinion.

They all exchanged glances. Chris was the first one to speak. "No, Neal, it was good, damn good, it just..." His voice trailed off as he searched for the right words.

"Sounded vaguely familiar." Johnson finished the sentence for him. I looked down at the page and quickly reread it.

"What? Like a rip-off?" I asked, taken aback by the perceived accusation. There was nothing that I disliked more than being accused of ripping off someone, plagiarizing.

"No, not like a rip-off." Chris quickly shot down the question knowing how insulting that could be. "More like, um..." He stopped again.

"It was kind of..." Now Johnson seemed to be struggling to describe his thoughts as well.

"Kind of what?" I asked.

Chris and Johnson looked at each other.

"Jesus, you guys are fucking pussies," Rich blurted out with anger in his voice. "It sounds like you are bitching about us."

Chris and Johnson nodded their heads emphatically.

"Really? That's weird," I said as I read over the poem searching for the lines and phrases that made them think that. "I honestly wasn't referring to you. I don't remember what I was referring to."

"Like you said before," Johnson said with subtle hints of doubt and malice in his voice.

"Neal, it's no big deal," Chris said. "When you write, you try to entice emotions in others, and that's what you have done. You've succeeded in the ultimate goal."

I shook my head, still in utter disbelief that they felt offended by 'Service Boy.' As I continued going through the words, Miss Claudia came by with our food.

"Here you go, boys," she said, putting the plates down in front of each of us. "I will be right back with more coffee for you. Is there anything else my boys need?" She looked around as we all shook our heads.

"Thank you, Miss Claudia," I said. She turned and walked away.

We ate in silence, giving me some time to reflect on my trip to New York. It was just over three years ago. I swung through the city for a couple of days to clear my head after...after what? A few weeks prior Johnson, Chris, and I had taken a trip to Atlantic City. Rich didn't come because he was helping a friend with a coke deal that earned him a couple thousand dollars he needed to pay off a gambling debt. Not that Rich really needed the money. He was more addicted to the excitement of being involved in the illegal transaction. It was the same reason he gambled and part of how he fell into the addiction that prompted us to be sitting in our booth again.

We had gone up to Atlantic City to fuck around and blow what little extra money we had. I had done all right, and the trip had paid for itself, but Johnson and Chris had broken the bank. I was driving them back when they asked to stop off in Trenton. The last time we were in Trenton, Johnson and I had met Kate. We both had a thing for her but decided for the sake of preserving our friendship that neither one of us would pursue her.

When we got to her house, Johnson immediately took her into her room and talked her into letting Chris and him stay for a few days so they could earn some money. After he had sealed the deal with her, he informed me of their plans and said that I could go on my way. It was then that I realized he wanted me gone so that he could win Kate. That's when I went to New York.

I didn't do much but stew while I was in New York. I was upset with all of my friends over those two days, probably a good explanation for why I don't like New York that much. I remembered walking around the Guggenheim, trying to be soothed by the pain and passion that was represented in the art surrounding me. While I was constantly moved by the amazing work that hung on the walls, I couldn't get the idea of Kate and Johnson out of my head. I had never worried about things like that before. If my friend wanted a girl, I would step aside. But Kate bothered me for some reason. It was a dagger, and I never fully understood why. After two days in New York, I drove home, and on the way 'Service Boy' spilled from my pen. I thought genius had appeared on the page, but I decided not to submit it. I wanted to keep it as a special poem for myself and for those I cared about.

I came back to the present and realized that Rich had also gone off into his own little world. He quietly sat across from me muttering the name, "Claire," over and over again.

"Hey!" I snapped my fingers in front of his face, waking him up from his daydream. He looked at me with embarrassed interest. "Who's Claire?"

Life filled his eyes. Slight color returned to the gray, and for a brief second, he didn't look like the junkie he'd become.

"She's the reason I'm quitting," he said, as though it was an obvious fact.

Our jaws dropped. To quit for anyone other than yourself was a faux pas that never worked. It was easy to be strong as long as things were good, but remembering the good times and feelings you had while using always came to the forefront of memories whenever things went wrong with the relationship. It was dangerous and foolish.

Chris, the most stunned out of all of us, said, "You're quitting for a woman?"

"No, no," Rich said. "I'm quitting for me. She made me realize that I need to."

The three of us threw tiny glances at each other until Johnson decided that he wasn't happy with the explanation. "What the fuck are you talking about?"

Rich lowered his head. I could tell that he didn't like reliving the memory. I almost told him that he didn't have to explain when he began.

"It was just a few years ago. I met Claire at a concert. I was so fucked up...imagine that." He smiled at his joke. "We continued to talk throughout the years and became good friends. Sometime in those years, I started to have feelings for her, but never acted on them because I kept..." He paused. The words were lost on him. Describing those moments in life is almost impossible. "...forgetting them, I guess would be the best way to put it," he said. "The more we talked, the stronger my feelings became, and in a single moment of sobriety about a year ago, I fell in love with her, I think."

A slight smile crossed his face. Not many people would have noticed it, but since he had only grimaced since we had been there, the mild upward shift in the corner of his lip was pretty monumental.

"That was the last time I saw her, or talked to her, until Friday," he said. "I don't remember where I was or what I was doing. I just know that I saw her there, and she didn't recognize me."

The smile faded, disappeared.

"She remembered me once I told her who I was," he said. "And all of my feelings emerged once again. I think I love her, but I don't feel anything, for anyone, ever." He looked at me. "That was when I called you," he said. "I have to feel so I know if I love her or not. Either way, no matter how I feel about Claire, I have to quit. So I can be the Rich of old before Michelle fucked me up these past few years."

Chris started to say something, but I stopped him. Now was not the time to argue over the cause of Rich's addictions. He knew he needed to quit. That was the important thing.

"I just," Rich paused, "I just have to know."

Then he went back into his own world, staring deeply into the laminate table-top.

Chris

Chris was born to former hippies turned entrepreneurs.

His father had marched against the Viet Nam war under Johnson, and his mother had marched against it under Nixon. After they married, they both gave up their liberal ways and turned over to the conservative side of life, and when Chris came into the picture, they decided it wasn't safe to raise young children on the harsh streets of Los Angeles. In an effort to give him a life away from violence, drugs, and gangs, they moved to Northern Virginia. The irony here never went unnoticed by Chris.

While most kids that Chris grew up with slept with teddy bears or random sporting equipment, Chris slept with a notebook and pen. Every morning when his mom woke him up, she would find ink all over his face and sheets. She tried taking the pen away from him, swearing that he couldn't have it back. But every night, he found another one and in the quiet of his room, scribbled out stories of witches and vampires. Witches and vampires who hunted children and ate their souls. His mom didn't approve of such violence and demanded that he change them. His horror story beginnings were altered to include witches and vampires that tickled children. It was their laughter that kept them alive. He learned young that editors don't always want to keep the writer's voice.

As Chris grew, his stories matured. His witches became lovelorn women, and his vampires became confused, searching men—all of his characters trying to find a place in this world where nothing is what it seems. He fell in and out of schools, never popular and rarely remembered by the other students who sat next to him in class. When he stopped showing up during his freshman year of college, Chris was certain that none of his classmates even noticed.

Chris and I met at a coffee shop when we were 18. He was sitting in the corner, heartbroken over the loss of his first love—a girl named Becky. Quietly muttering incoherent lines of heartbreak and pain, he caught me peeking over his shoulder at the poem he was writing.

"Do you like it?" he asked. He didn't seem to mind my eavesdropping.

"Yeah, I do. How long did it take you to write it?"

"I didn't write it," he said. "My pen did. I just held it upright."

We became friends instantly. On that first day of friendship, we talked about how every page had a story, every pen was fated to write a certain poem, and how the writer simply found it. We talked for hours, about Becky, about writing, and about the moon. Chris had an obsession with the moon. A few years in the future, Chris would get a moon tattoo in between his shoulder blades.

Chris had scribbled "2:30 a.m." all over the margins of his notebook so I had to ask what it was for. He smiled as he recited the words, "May Venus always shine bright, pain never be as real as it feels, sunsets last two minutes and thirty-six seconds, and the moon never be as beautiful as she is at 2:30 a.m."

I asked him what it meant, but his only response was that some memories are meant to be private.

We spent the rest of that day together and went to the diner that night. It was the first of our many late-night writing sessions, a night of discovery and discussion. We found that debates and healthy conversation came easily between the two of us. And so our saga began. Chris, heartbroken and alone in the world and me, wondering what love was and searching for a true friend.

IV.

I slept on Rich's couch that night. Between the nauseating odors emitting from the cushions and Rich's moaning and throaty, phlegmy coughing, I did not have a very restful night. Around 4:30 AM, I got up from the couch to check on Rich. He was curled up in the fetal position, shivering. The sheets were clinging to his body from the sweat that poured off of his back and chest. As I stood in his doorway, he cried out with a wail of torture and pain. He cringed and pulled his body tighter into the tiny ball that he had formed. I shook my head and shut his door. This night would certainly be the hardest. I was glad I could be there for him if he needed me.

I remembered my own experience of this night only vaguely—the shivers, the shakes, the vomiting, all happening at the same time and separately. I sweat so much I couldn't keep myself hydrated. It took every ounce of self-control to not score again. I almost broke many times that night. It seemed like an eternity, like I would eternally experience such disgusting misery. It was the worst night of my life.

I went back to the couch, and knowing it was pointless, I tried to fall asleep. As I listened to Rich's misery, memories of my past life came rushing back, and with the painful memories of my own withdrawal, I also realized I was starting to miss the drugs. I wanted to score. Just one more time. I knew I could keep it hidden from Rich while he was going through his withdrawals, and I had no doubt that I would be able to quit again, at least that's what I told myself. At some point, I finally admitted to myself that I was being absurd, but some part of me still wanted to score. It was a fucked up night.

I still hadn't fallen asleep when Chris called me the next morning. I reached down and grabbed my phone.

"Hello?" I said, trying to sound as groggy as possible.

"Neal, it's Chris. Where's Rich?" he asked.

"Still asleep," I said. "He'll probably be out until three or so."

"You want to meet me for breakfast?"

"Sure, the diner?" I asked.

"No, Café 28. They have better hash browns."

Chris had asked me to meet him at the diner many times before. He had never asked me to meet him at Café 28. I didn't think his pallet for hash browns had grown so extensively that he really wanted the Café 28 version as opposed to any others. I assumed something was off.

"I'll be there in 15," I said and hung up the phone. I couldn't remember the last time I took my contacts out, and my eyes were killing me. I stood up and peered into a mirror hanging on the wall, gazing into my tired, bloodshot eyes. Rich had purchased the mirror at the

Stewart's Brewing House in Edinburgh, Scotland years ago, back before Chris and Michelle had helped point him down the path that he was currently attempting to stray from. Rich used to get high off of traveling to areas of the world he had never seen before. Then he met Lady H and Mr. C. After that, he never traveled. A year ago, I tried to get him to come with me to Seattle, but he said he had no interest in seeing it. That was when I knew he was gone.

I stared at myself in the mirror and wondered if there was anything I could have done to prevent his decline. I shook my head as I came up short.

"Nobody can change somebody else's personally chosen path," I decided. I grabbed my keys and ran out the door to my car.

When I got to Café 28, Chris was already there. Two cups of coffee were sitting on the table, and Chris was smoking a cigarette. I sat down across from him and lit one for myself.

"I already ordered for you. Hope you don't mind," he said.

"No, it's all good," I said. "What did I order?"

"Western omelet, extra hash browns."

"Sounds good to me."

Chris was nervously smoking his cigarette, tapping it on the ashtray every few seconds, making its cherry bright and pointed. His eyes looked down towards the table, not up at mine.

"It was good to have all of us together again last night," he said in a distant voice.

"Yeah, it was." I was impatiently waiting to find out why he wanted to meet me here.

"I thought that you and Johnson would have had more to say to each other," he said. "You know, because of the Kate thing."

"Why did you want me to meet you here, Chris?" I asked, annoyed.

He finally looked up at me, his eyes lost in a sea of confusion. He looked like he needed to release feelings and emotions that he had kept bottled up inside for years. He was trying to escape himself.

While Chris was struggling with his demons, the waitress came by, dropped off the food, and warmed up our coffee. Chris's eyes looked down at his omelet and hash browns and then quickly jetted off to the left. I watched him blink back some tears, trying to hide his emotions. I suddenly noticed dark circles around his eyes, a mild shake to his hands. I closed my eyes and shook my head. "Jesus, Chris. How long have you been back on?"

"Is it that obvious?" he asked, his voice full of shame.

"I figured it out in, what? Two minutes? Yes, it's fucking obvious. How long?"

"I don't remember," he said. "Six, maybe eight months."

"How did this happen?"

"I just needed it. I couldn't deal with anything anymore. It started small and just kept growing."

I stared at him in disbelief. He was one of the strongest advocates of quitting, yet here I was, sitting across from him as he was tweaking out and in need of a fix.

"You know how it is," he said. "I thought it was a one time thing, and the next thing I knew I was buying every day, needing more and more to get to the same point. I couldn't stop."

I leaned my head back, hitting it repeatedly against the wall behind me. "Aw, you fucking hypocrite. What the hell are you doing?"

"I don't know anymore," he said, still fighting the tears. "I *am* a fucking hypocrite."

His eyes stared into mine. They were blank and empty. Chris stood at the crossroads that all of us had hit at one point—one road would lead him back to Junkie-town, and the other would take him back to Sobriety-ville. I knew the path he wanted to take, but I also knew that he had a weak soul.

"What happened?" I asked, shaking my head.

"It started a year and a half ago, while you were in Arizona." His eyes darted into every direction as he talked. "I was sitting at a bar, working on my new story...the last story I started. I was writing feverishly, and my pen was spilling words of, what I would consider, pure brilliance. I sat there for what may have been hours, lost in a notebook of blank pages, each page opening up new doors of possibility for the story. At some point, somebody tapped me on the shoulder. I turned around and..." He took a deep breath and shut his eyes for a second. "And Becky was there," he continued. "I was lost. I never thought that I would see her again, and there she was, smiling at me. She was still as beautiful as the day...whatever. I'm not going to recite the same regurgitated crap everyone always says. Needless to say, everything I ever felt about her came back in that moment. We talked for a little while, just normal catching up bullshit. Then she said it." He paused for a minute, filling me with anticipation.

"Said what?" I asked.

"She told me that it was because I spent so much time and exerted so much of my potential on writing, and not enough on school or a career, that she broke up with me."

I nodded and breathed out, "So you started using again."

He glared at me, his eyes shooting needles of anger.

"No," he said, matter of factly. "I quit writing, and I started working toward a career, a respectable profession, so I could make money and be able to, one day, support a family. That was when Rich and I got into that fight. It didn't matter to me though. All I wanted was to show Becky that I could hold a respectable job. That I could support her. I wanted to finally grow up and be a man."

"You don't have to have a 'real job' to be a man," I said. "That is dependent on your character."

"I understand that," he said. "But I wanted to show her, to prove myself. I figured it would bring me one step closer to being with her."

It was pathetic, really. At least six years had passed since they had broken up, but still when he thought of her he was taken back to the days they had together. He remembered the love he had for her and how much it hurt when they broke up. This was not the first time he changed his life in an attempt to get back together with her. We had all grown tired of this excessively played out movie. It never worked and only made him more and more miserable.

"So there I was, Chris Franklyn, working a nine to five, going to bed before midnight. Hell, the only time I picked up a pen was to sign my name to a check to pay my bills, on time. Becky and I kept in contact for the next year. She constantly told me how proud of me she was, and how if I had been doing this back when we were together, we'd still be together." He shook his head as he realized his own futility. "And then...six months ago, she told me she was getting married."

His voice cracked on that last word, and he had to stop talking.

"Gotcha," was all I could think of to say.

"She never even told me she was dating someone," he said as he picked up his fork and started poking at his food. I followed suit and scooped up a forkful of hash browns. I crammed them into my mouth, and my eyes widened. They were the best damn hash browns I had ever had. "Damn, these are a lot better than the diner's!"

"Told ya," he said.

Chris picked at his food while I shoveled mine into my mouth. I felt like I hadn't eaten in weeks. The stress of Rich and now Chris had taken a lot out of me. I needed to refuel, and those hash browns were just the thing.

"I felt bad for calling Rich a junkie yesterday," Chris said quietly as his fork prodded his food.

"Don't worry about it. He doesn't know," I said, my mouth full of western omelet. "And I won't tell him."

"I appreciate that, Neal." He took a bite then with a look of disgust, he put down his fork and forcibly swallowed.

"What story were you working on?" I asked.

"When?"

"A year and a half ago. When you saw Becky."

"It was called 'Orange Moon.'"

"You have a week to finish it," I said, still cramming food into my mouth.

"Why?"

I took the last bite from my plate, picked up my napkin, and calmly wiped my mouth.

"If you don't, I kick your ass."

As we left Café 28, Chris walked with me to my car.

"What are we doing today?" he asked.

"I think that I will deal with you first. You'll be easier."

He looked at me confused. "How do you figure that?"

I reached back and swung as hard as I could, my fist connecting squarely with his jaw. He dropped to the ground and gripped his face with his hands. I pulled my hand back and rubbed my sore knuckles. That was the first time I had ever punched someone. It hurt my hand more than I expected. Reaching out, I offered him my hand. He took it, and I pulled him up off the ground. He rubbed his jaw, but he was smiling when he looked at me.

"Thanks," he said, stretching his mouth in an illogical attempt to ease the pain. "What do we do for Rich?"

"Tonight," I said with a smile, "we burn."

Diary Entry III:

Dear Jack,

The smoke rings of life drift upward, disappearing into the atmosphere like so many forgotten souls of the past. I can't help but wonder if I will be one of those souls. Especially in the eyes of Claire, the mystical beauty I met at the 9:30 Club last night.

It was a good show for only $12.00. I got to see four bands, none of which are big in name but all turned out to be large in talent. I arrived just moments before the first band played their set, and as soon as I walked into the club, I saw her. I don't know if it was all the weed that I had smoked, or all the beer I had imbibed before the show, but she had this brilliant glow about her. She shone like the full moon at 2:30 AM. Chris and Michelle followed me in, distracting my attention away from the personification of Venus in front of me. By the time I turned around, she had vanished, like those smoke rings.

I stumbled into the crowd with Chris and Michelle close behind. We were all in a similar state of mind. As I hate to be the third wheel, I tried to escape them, but Chris, trying to escape Michelle, stayed close behind me. I scurried, ducked, and weaved my way through the crowd in search of my angel.

When the first band came on stage, I walked right into the crowd and found myself face to face with Claire. Our eyes locked, and my passion for her burned eternal, like a Yule log. She gave me a little wink, and as the band started to play, I moved closer to her. Soon we were holding hands and dancing. I was in heaven. Complete freedom had found me as we bonded beautifully. Our bodies meshed and connected as one. Just before the band finished playing, she kissed me.

I must rank her in the top five of my eternally long list. Moist but not wet, firm but soft, tight without the pinched lips. It was perfect. I could no longer feel the heat of the club or the sweat that was spraying off of everyone jumping around me. I was transported to a more beautiful place, a place where only she and I stood, a slight drizzle hitting our faces as we expressed devotion for one another.

I think that we only stopped to breathe after that. For three bands we shared a moment, a very long moment, but it wasn't nearly long enough. As the crowd dissipated and the ringing in my ears started to subside, I looked at her and was still in awe of her beauty.

I requested to see her again, and with a look and a wink that I will never forget, she took my hand, wiped the sweat off on her jeans, and wrote her number on it. She lightly bit her lip, (God it just kills me when girls do that) and said, "I can't wait to hear from you." Then she turned and walked away through the crowd. When I realized that I didn't know her name, I called, "Hey! Who are you?"

She looked back at me and smiled again. She shouted "Claire!"

My Venus was named.

Now I look forward to the day that I see her again. Hell, I just can't wait to hear her voice.

Well, good night, my brother, and sleep well. Tomorrow brings new life to a less drab day. Possibly all my dreams come true.

From one subterranean to another,

Rich Stevens

V.

When Chris and I arrived back at Rich's, Johnson was already there. He was sitting on the couch, watching TV, and talking on the phone. As we walked into the living room, he sat up real quick and nervously ran his hand through his dark, mop-like hair.

"Yeah, yeah," he said in a hushed voice. "You too, talk to you soon."

He hung up the phone and stood to greet us. "What's up, guys?"

Chris shook his head and grunted an indecipherable comment while rubbing his jaw. I glanced at him and muttered, "Nothing."

"He up yet?" Chris shouted from the kitchen while foraging for ice.

"No, not yet," Johnson said, his eyes shooting nervously between the entrance to the kitchen and me. "What's on the agenda for tonight?"

I pulled a bottle of lighter fluid out of my pocket and tossed it to him. He let it drop to the floor as he looked at it. Chris came from around the corner with an ice-filled towel pressed to his jaw.

"Tonight, we burn," he declared proudly, though slightly muffled from the towel.

Johnson stared at him. "What the fuck happened to you?"

"Neal hit me," Chris said nonchalantly.

"What?" Johnson cried. His eyes turned to glare at me with all the rage he had been hiding. "Why the fuck did you do that?"

I was leaning over the table reading the headlines on a paper from a month before. I looked over casually, straight into his eyes.

"'Cause he deserved it."

Johnson took a step closer to me. "Who are you, judge and jury?"

"Yes," I said, nodding my head. I'm not sure if it was because I hadn't gotten much sleep the night before, or maybe I had too much coffee at breakfast, or maybe every jaded and malicious opinion I had about him all crashed into each other, but I was ready to kill him if I had to.

Johnson took another step closer, staring down at me. I could smell cigarettes on his breath. He was breathing heavily, his nostrils violently flaring. His eyes followed mine, his hands clenched into fists. I knew he was waiting for the opportune moment to take a swing at me.

"Johnson, I did deserve..." Chris started to say.

"Shut up, Chris." I cut him off. "He's not going to hit me."

Johnson's face transformed from anger into a look of shock, as if I had insulted him.

"I'm not?" he asked.

"No, you aren't," I smirked, standing up straight, attempting to meet his eyes on a more even level.

"Why do you say that?"

"I'm not going to let you."

Johnson's right arm pulled back. I continued to stand perfectly still with a smirk on my face, watching him intently.

"Will you two fucking grow up?" Rich's voice cut through the room.

Johnson turned his head to see Rich standing in his doorway. Quickly I swung and caught him in the jaw, sending him to the floor. A cheap shot, I knew, but a much deserved one. The second time I had ever hit someone was far more satisfying than the first. At the rate they were coming, I might have a good deal of practice by the end of the day. I jumped on top of his body, pinning his right arm down with my left hand and his left arm with my knee. I pulled my fist back to hit him again.

"Why the fuck are you pissed at me?" I screamed. "What the fuck did I do to you? You have no right to be mad at me. Stop being a fucking asshole. You should only be mad at yourself. Grow the fuck up before I really hurt you."

I stood up and took a step back, looking at him on the ground.

"I'm not mad at you," I explained, calmer now. "I'm pissed at the situation, I'm pissed I lost. I'm pissed I lost to you. Two years on the road helped me start to get over it. I still am getting over it. But you, you have no right to be mad at me. I didn't do anything wrong."

I looked around at Chris and Rich and suddenly felt bad. Quietly I said, "But we're not here for me, we're here for Rich. So let's put this behind us for now and be his friend. We don't have to speak to each other again if you don't want to, but we do have to be here for him."

I offered him my hand. After a long dirty look, he took it and I pulled him up. Chris handed Johnson the ice pack he had been using. Johnson snatched it out of his hand and put it against his jaw.

"Jesus, it's like living with two infants," Rich said, as he walked into the room. "And you two don't even live here."

He patted Johnson on the chest, letting him know that everything was okay, that it was time to let it go. He slowly walked through the room and spied the bottle of lighter fluid on the floor. A slight chuckle left his mouth.

"Tonight, we burn," he said quietly. A slight smile spread on his face as he sat down on the couch. He looked around at the four of us. "Guys, I feel better today. It was a rough night, but I feel better."

"Why so?" Chris asked.

Rich looked at him. "'Cause it's the four of us again. This is what I need. The four of us can achieve anything together." He smiled a weak smile. Chris sat down next to him, and Rich turned to look at him.

"What the fuck happened to your face?"

"Neal hit me."

"Damn, Neal," he said, and he looked at me. "Angry much today?"

"Just suffering from a severe and debilitating lack of sleep," I said with a slight smile.

Rich laughed to himself and let out a loud, satisfied sigh as he stretched his arms and back. An audible crack came from every joint in his body and echoed off the walls. The toxins that had been stored within every free space in his body were definitely being shaken.

"So, where do we start?" he asked after a moment of shaking off the initial feeling of the drugs reentering his system.

Chris and I walked into the bedroom with Rich and Johnson on our heels. I took a look around to assess the situation. It wasn't pretty. The carpets were stained from nights of piss, shit, and vomit hitting the ground wherever Rich, or whoever, passed out and never properly cleaned up. The smell was terrible. We had a lot of work ahead of us.

"Rich," I put my hand on his shoulder, "you still have cash, right?"

He looked at me and started to laugh.

"Good," I said. "Rip the sheets off your bed. They go first. After that, you're going to have to do something very hard. You have to go through all your letters and pictures and get rid of any that remind you of that life. Anything you wrote about it, anything you read that would remind you of it. It'll be very difficult, and you will hate it, but it needs to be done."

Rich nodded. "I can do it. Y'all are here, I can do anything right now." He headed to the bed and started taking off the sheets and Chrisress cover. The Chrisress was stained with different colored spots—some were very recognizable, like the nights Rich wet himself, but there were also blood spots that raised questions none of us wanted to ask. I felt certain he wouldn't want to talk about it, that was if he remembered what happened.

"Chris, go through and find any razor blades, needles, bent spoons, cut straws. You know what to look for. Anything that you wouldn't want in your house, find it. Then I want you to throw them all away."

"Cool," Chris said as he walked out of the room to look for trash bags.

I looked at Johnson. He was watching me with great interest, waiting to hear what shit job I gave him.

"Rich," I called over my shoulder looking Johnson in the eye. "How do you feel about hardwood?"

"Whatever," he said.

I smiled at Johnson. He had already started shaking his head.

"Johnson, you and I rip up carpet."

Diary Entry IV:

Dear Jack,

As the years pass, I find myself growing angrier, lost in a sea of distrust and hatred. I started using coke in order to keep myself awake during the day, when all I wanted to do was sleep until Armageddon. Fascinating drug that is, coke. It brings out emotions and feelings that I didn't know I had. I feel like I'm searching for a lost soul that I can never get back. I'm afraid to wake up when I'm asleep, and afraid to fall asleep when awake.

Sorry to do this during our time, but I have to get this down now.

Mike lived next door
we used to play
together in the backyard.
I used to let him
beat the shit out of me.
He moved away
10 years ago.
I shot him today.
His chest exploded,
blood spraying like
a red meteor shower.

His eyes rolled back
into his head,
and his mouth
changed into a grimace.
I didn't see anything
after that.
I turned and walked away.
I came back to my place,
prepared my needle,
and shot it in my vein.
I forgot my life,
my past and my future.
The anger that I store
gets its release—
twice tonight.
I've asked to be
delivered from evil,
but was led to the
valley of sin.
My parents showed me love,
with the backside of a hand.
A night of drinking
meant a night of pain.
Sunday family dinner
was a chance to be
reminded of how worthless I was.
The day of the crash
was the day I believed
dreams can come true.
I was put into foster homes

where cigarettes were
put out on me.
I just shrugged
at the pain
and savored the scars.
When they moved away
I knew that dreams
could come true.
I was out on my own
at the age of 15
no one to trust
no one to love.
I sold myself
on the streets to men.
Some were married,
some were nice,
some were mean.
Spent some time upstate,
for petty little things.
A robbery here,
a possession there.
I was a "small time thug."
Many times the state
went easy on me
because of my past.
I've had my share of women.
They mainly felt sorry for me,
until they got to know me.
She showed me what love was,
and how someone really cared.

The day she left me
I realized that
dreams can come true.
I have snorted coke,
and shot smack,
tripped away many nights,
and smoked my mind to mush.
I've been stabbed and beaten,
kicked and battered,
and whatever they've done
I can see
dreams that can come true.
I've never met anyone that I liked,
but many that I loathed.
I've lived on the street,
in a box,
on a bench,
and in my dreams.
I've never known
what a home was
but have dreamed
of them at times.
I have prayed
to the Father
asking for one,
but every day
I wake up,
wondering if
dreams can come true.

See what I mean? What the fuck is that? I need some sleep, but I'm afraid to. It's 2:30 A.M. Jack, do I know where my mind is?

From one subterranean to another,

Rich Stevens

VI.

Chris was walking through Rich's apartment with a trash bag already filled half-way with syringes, straws that had been cut to two inches, razor blades, pocket mirrors, and other paraphernalia. Rich was sitting in his closet going through shoeboxes of pictures and old writings he had stored over his lifetime.

Occasionally, he came across a picture or a poem that caused him to sweat and shake. He would stand up, violently throw it across the room, and storm outside until he became calm again. Every time this happened, Johnson glared at me, as if to say, "he shouldn't be doing this yet." I ignored him and focused on pulling up the carpet, watching over my shoulder to see if Rich had returned.

Following one of these episodes, Rich came back to his closet drenched in sweat. His eyes were bloodshot and puffy; his hands were shaking so badly, he couldn't even hold a piece of paper. I took a break from the carpet and went over to him, closing the closet door behind me.

I sat down next to him. "How ya doing, buddy?"

"Why do I have to do this?" he asked. I could tell that he had been crying. His voice still had that quiver. "I can't do this, Neal. I want to break. I want to crack. I can't do this. I'm not ready."

"I know it's hard, Rich, but you have to get rid of anything that will remind you of that time," I said apologetically. I could see the pain in his eyes and felt horrible for putting him through the torture that he was feeling. "Rich, if there were an easier way I would have you do that instead…"

"Why can't you do this? And let me rip up carpet?" he begged.

"I'll show you why," I said as I picked up the shoebox and threw it all into a trash bag. "I'm done."

"Alright," he said, with a hint of understanding in his voice. "I hate you right now, but I'll respect you in the morning."

"Just like every girl you've ever slept with," I said.

He tried to crack a smile, but it came across as a grimace. I stood and squeezed his shoulder for support.

"You're doing fine, man. Keep at it."

He nodded and pulled the shoebox out of the trash bag.

I went back to the carpet. I pulled a corner up, grabbed the razorblade, and cut it before throwing it onto the pile Johnson and I had created. I pulled out a cigarette and lit it. Wiping the sweat off my forehead, I moved to another corner. Johnson was moving the bed to the area that was now hardwood when he asked, "Why the sheets?"

"Well, every time you lie down to go to bed at night, everything that you have done that day gets transferred to the sheets. Through your sweat, saliva, semen, whatever," I explained. "So when you rip the sheets off the bed and burn them, you, in a sense, burn the essence of all those things."

He thought about it for a second and then asked, "Why not just wash them?"

"Well," I smiled. "I'm assuming you've slept with a skank before, right?"

He nodded.

"How many washes did it take to get her smell out of your sheets?" I asked.

Finally, he broke a smile. "Quicker to burn them."

"Exactly."

We went back to work on ripping out the carpet. I could hear Chris talking to himself out in the hallway. He kept repeating the same line over and over again. Constantly I would hear the phrase, "Ahhh, love," being said in different ways, with different emphases and accents. I chose to ignore it, but it had become increasingly annoying.

After a minute, Johnson heard it too. He glanced out to the hallway and then back at me. I shrugged and continued working. Suddenly the collective consciousness that we once shared began to fall back upon us as Chris burst into the room, screaming, "I'VE GOT IT!!!"

Rich crawled out of the closet and sat against the wall; Johnson and I turned and sat down—all attention on Chris, who was grinning from ear to ear.

"Ahhh, love," he started. "What a splendid…" He paused and had a look of doubt on his face. "…thing. Having traveled down this road once or twice before I know of only one certainty: 'nothing is definite.' A tender kiss, a passionate hug, a loving fuck, all things that can disappear in a second's notice.

Pain is a much more experienced emotion and is usually a direct result of love. The scent of a certain incense wafting through the air reminds us of a loved one from the past. Memories repeat and emotions resurface, all climaxing to a point higher and beyond anything one has experienced before. You smoke your cigarettes, drink your booze, and spend your nights watching Internet porn, paying with your soul to wallow in your loneliness. You eat your narcotics in pathetic attempts to climb higher than the pain, but crashing like a shooting comet, plummeting through space and time on a roller coaster of sadness and depression, waiting for those few moments of bliss that are forgotten like yesterday's hot band, stuck in the drawer with the rest of your CDs hoping for the next time to be opened.

But tomorrow never comes.

Stuck in the deepest depths of your emotional dungeon, you befriend others of your sort. Friends chiseling their way out of the prison of solitude, searching for another lost soul to comfort them, waiting for a day that someone will once again make you smile. You share a cocoon with these emotional pariahs and before the realization hits, you've tunneled through the wall holding the hand of another who couldn't leave the luggage behind, and a strong bond forms between the two of you. A friendly kiss, an occasional hug, and an emotionless fuck take place to help defuse the wick that is wired to the time bomb of depression and hours of masturbation. The wick grows shorter each time and the sparks, grander than a new year's night, begin to fly and jump and soar around the two of you until you find yourself right back at the beginning of the story.

Ahhh, love."

The four of us erupted. The powerful, energetic delivery sent us all into a frenzy, and soon we were all standing in a circle throwing out tidbits of poetry, ideas for stories, monologues, and the like. Our brains were feeding off of each other's, and for hours we prodded the deepest crevasses, looking, searching for the next great creation that we could be proud to have witnessed. It was an amazing event that only came every once in a while. It was incredible to have it back that day.

Even Rich seemed to forget the pain that was permeating through every cell of his body. He was able to remember who he once was–a writer, a poet, an artist, and a friend. His face almost looked like the Rich of old, full of life and vigor, as lyrics for sonnets dripped from his tongue. The emptiness that was renting space in his eyes was out for lunch as his laughter became the laughter of a man guided by passion and hope for a life worth living.

Diary Entry V:

Dear Jack,

Every time I try to eat something my stomach feels like it is filled with lead. I don't remember the last time I weighed this much. I went to Burger King the other day and ordered two cheeseburgers off the dollar menu but could only eat half of one. I don't get it. I used to eat like it was my job, but recently it's felt like a chore. I can tell I'm hungry, but I can't bring myself to put anything down. The only thing that keeps me trying is the fact that I know I need to eat. I'm not a supermodel after all, or at least not yet. I'll talk to you later, brother. Friend just showed up with drugs and food.

From one subterranean to another,
Rich Stevens

VII.

By the time we had finished, only the furniture remained in Rich's house. We even threw out most of his old clothes. I suggested taking the nasty couch with us, but Rich decided he would buy a new one and have the deliverymen take it out.

"It would be easier that way," he explained. I had to agree. My car was a small two-door and Chris had a sedan, perfect for a businessman taking clients out, not so much a mover hauling furniture to light on fire.

We loaded every ounce of garbage into my car, leaving only enough room for Rich and myself. Chris and Johnson followed us in Chris's car.

We headed out to the abandoned baseball field that had since been disguised by a forest full of trees. The drive was long and consisted of windy gravel roads, which no person in their right mind would want to take, especially at night. Every S in the road was followed by a blind turn or a hidden drive. When traversing the dangerous road at 25 miles per hour, terrified drivers often mistook a shadow or bush seen out of the corner of the eye as a deer or other forest animal bounding into the road, causing them to swerve into ditches, trees, and guardrails.

Naturally, we were driving 45 miles per hour.

Rich didn't say a word the entire drive. He stared out the window, I'm sure, searching for validation on what we had just done. An entire life had been cut up, ripped out, crumpled, torn, broken off, and thrown into plastic trash bags that now resided in the back seat of a car. The hardest part was yet to come. He realized that and was terrified.

When we arrived at the ball field, the four of us started hauling the bags of a heavy, vile-smelling, putrid existence toward one of the fields. We dumped Rich's life out onto the pitcher's mound. As the pile grew, Rich's eyes begged for absolution. The last few years of his life were laid out before him, as though he was meeting his maker. Today was his judgment day, but instead of being tried by a higher power, he was the judge.

Once everything was emptied, each of us pulled out two bottles of lighter fluid and slowly walked around the pile, squirting the flammable liquid on every memory. We moved slowly, methodically, with a purpose, attempting to savor the moment and all that it stood for. This was not an act to be done hastily but instead with precision. It was not every day we destroyed a life. Glances shot across the pile, each face a picture of stoicism and fear, a little excitement hidden in the eyes.

With the garbage drenched, Chris reached into his pocket, pulled out a book of matches, and handed them to Rich. Taking the matches, Rich cradled them in his hand, staring down, lost in a fog of thoughts. When one wants to forget something, it is impossible not to remember. In a power surge of memories and emotion, Rich's brain was lost in the past, far from where we stood in the present moment.

The four of us endured in silence as Rich dealt with every demon that haunted his thoughts. I could see from across the circle that he had started to cry. Tears rolled down his face and dripped off his chin, landing on the ground where they were immediately absorbed into the soil. His eyes moved away from the matches and turned to me. I could see the fear and the sadness that filled them. For a moment I thought he might not be ready for this. I dreaded that I had pushed him too far, too fast.

After another moment of internal meditation, a mild smirk crossed his face, and I knew he was going to be fine.

As though in slow motion, he opened the matchbook with one hand, selected a single match, and bent it around the bottom of the book so that the match head rested on the igniter. With a deep inhale, he placed his thumb on the match head and dragged it across the igniter, sparking the flame to life. The flame grew higher as he turned the matchbook until the entire book was on fire. With an exhale that could only symbolize the release of everything holding him in his spiraling drain of pain and addiction, he tossed the burning matchbook onto life as he knew it.

The flame erupted into a magnificent display of oranges, reds, greens, and purples. The scent of burning lighter fluid filled the air around us as the smoke of papers and plastics rose into sky. Our faces became illuminated in the dark, clear night. The shadows parried and thrust around us in the eternal battle of light and dark. All of our eyes filled with excitement and joy as we watched the flames grow higher. The heat licked the sky, and the warmth acted as our mutual baptism, with Rich receiving the greatest redemption. As the purple haze climbed upward, Rich could do nothing but smile.

"Ahhh, love," he said, giving Chris a little wink.

"Ahhh, love," the rest of us said in unison.

"Ahhh, love," I thought.

I've loved many things in my lifetime, but never have I had the honor of loving a woman. I had been with my fair share and had loved for a night but never for longer than that. My last "relationship" was with this girl named Cindy. We met in Pasadena, California, at a bar on Colorado Boulevard. She had long, dark hair and eyes that appeared to be violet–she swore she didn't wear contacts. Her red lips sat playfully on her face and moved ever so cautiously as she asked me questions and told me about her life and dreams. We danced and drank until the bar closed, and then we went back to my hotel.

This went on for a week. Every night we went to a different bar then back to the hotel where we would fuck like bunnies until the sun came up. Then she went home, promising to see me the next night. At the end of the week, she told me her boyfriend was coming back to town, and she wouldn't be able to see me the next night. We went through our ritual, and that morning when she left, I knew I would never see her again. So I left.

That was six months before I came back to Virginia for Rich. There had been others, but their names held little importance. It was mutual masturbation with most of them. Cindy was the last one I wanted to remember. She was the last one that involved feelings. She was the only one I remember feeling anything for.

Rich called my name, breaking me from my daydream, as he and the others headed to the cars. I shook my head, trying to clear the memories and ran to catch up with the guys.

That night we all went back to Rich's place for a celebration of sobriety. The burning had been a victory for all four of us, each taking our own inspiration from it. Johnson and Chris were on the couch, notebooks and pens our own inspiration from it. Johnson and Chris were on the couch, notebooks and pens in hand, working feverishly. Rich had tried to write, but his hands weren't working for him so he recited and I wrote for him. Every so often I would get an idea of my own and quickly summarize it in the margins so I could come back to it later.

"Hey, Neal," Rich said quietly, after finishing a line.

I stopped writing and looked up at him. He motioned for me to follow him into his room. I stood up and went after him. He shut the door behind me.

"What's up, kid?" I asked.

Rich disappeared into his closet and emerged a moment later with a book in hand. The black leather cover was trimmed in gold, and it had a black strap tying it shut. The pages were off-white, almost yellow. They were bent and dog-eared. I didn't have to ask. I already knew what it was.

"Umm, when I was going through all my shit, I came across this, and while I could chuck pretty much everything else, I can't bear to get rid of this."

I nodded. "That's okay. I never said that you had to throw everything away."

"I know," he said as his fingers lightly ran over the binding. His eyes began to well up with tears. "But I can't keep this. It's funny… Everything I threw out, I probably could have kept it all here, and it never would have bothered me. But the one thing I hang on to is the one thing I can't keep."

Carefully, I took the diary away from him. His fingers tried to hold onto it for as long as possible before they finally gave up.

"How about I hang on to this until you're ready to have it back?"

Rich closed his eyes and nodded. A tear rolled down his cheek and fell to the floor. Then he pulled me in and hugged me. I think he didn't want me to see him cry, but I could feel the tears as they dampened my shoulder. I hugged him back and kept repeating, "It'll be okay."

Rich and I came out of the bedroom after he had some time to compose himself after handing me the diary he just couldn't let go of. The four of us all sat around the apartment writing and talking about the night's events, laughing and joking around like the days of old. A few times Rich would go silent or get a series of chills that incapacitated him for extended periods of time.

After one of these episodes, he decided he was too tired to continue and went to bed. Johnson, Chris and I stayed up most of the night writing. I continually checked in on Rich. He hit a couple of rough patches throughout the night but nothing severe. A few times he called out to nameless faiths with muffled wails, and he still sweat with a fervor that soaked his sheets. I sat in the room, making sure he didn't involuntarily vomit, until it seemed the episode was over. Watching him closely, I found myself praying, even though I never really believed in a god. I prayed that he would be okay, that he would get through this. I prayed that the pain that was so evident on his face would soon subside.

It was strange to watch someone cry in his sleep.

Diary Entry VI:

Dear Jack,
>You know...fuck it.
>From one subterranean to another,
>Rich Stevens

IIX.

It's February.
    There is no reason to stay awake,
    yet no reason to sleep.
    The locusts eat the crops,
    the children eat the will to live,
    there are no permanent solutions.
    Demons disguised in white,
    infiltrate the domicile.
    Necessity is no longer needed.
    A shock to the heart can revive me.
    Why does everyone lie?
    Let me be your service boy.
    How immature can I be?
    More than you.
    I should sleep,
    but there is no point.
    Speed down Mulholland
    at midnight.
    I'll see you in heaven,
    unless you're in the hand basket,
    then I'll watch you in hell.
    Trust is gone,

belief is of the past.
Everything is lost.
Hope is all the future has,
and I want to die young.
The youths will never be good leaders.
She lied, he lied, you lied, I lied.
When is it okay to tell the truth?
I'm tired of being good.
Let's go kill someone,
anyone you want, I don't care.
Oh, wait, not him,
no, not her either.
This country is on its last leg,
I hope I'm gone before it is.
I like having land under my feet.
What the hell is this all about?

It wasn't the greatest thing that I had ever written, but it was the first thing I had put down on paper in a week. I looked around the living room. Chris was asleep in the armchair, curled up tight trying to fit all of his body on the single cushion. Johnson was sprawled out on the floor, his head resting on a notebook open to a half-filled page. I leaned over the armrest to see if Rich's door was still shut. It was.

I put the notebook on the coffee table and got up to go to the bathroom. I hadn't slept much the night before. In fact I hadn't slept much since I had come back to Virginia. I could feel it starting to take its toll on me, but for some reason I just couldn't fall asleep.

I came back out to the living room, and Rich was sitting on the couch reading my last poem. I stood there watching him as he mouthed the words. He nodded as he finished it, tossed the notebook on the table, and then looked up.

"Hey," he said. His eyes were still red from sleep, and his hands shook from a lack of nourishment.

"You like?" I asked. I took a seat next to him on the couch.

"Wasn't really reading it."

I rubbed my eyes. "I think the lack of sleep is getting to me."

"Starting to feel numb?"

"A bit." I stared at the ceiling and started to count the indentations in the paint. I soon realized it was a futile task and decided the appropriate number was infinity.

"I'll make some coffee," Rich said, standing up. He stepped over Johnson's body and walked toward the kitchen.

"You know what, Neal?" he called out.

"What's that, kid?" I asked as I picked up the notebook and scanned the poem.

"Dying is a lot more fun than coming back to life," he said, and then he disappeared through the kitchen doors.

It had been years since my last serious withdrawal, but I remembered it like I only just got through it. The cold sweat, the clammy, shaky hands, the dry mouth–all of these things were easy to deal with, but the brain does some fucked up shit during a withdrawal. You become convinced of things that were never real. You remember things that were never said, things that never happened, just so you can justify what is happening to you at that moment. You see things that aren't there, things that actually don't exist. I remember looking through my apartment asking myself what I could sell just so I could get a little taste. I remember picking through the fibers of the carpet to see if I spilled any, just enough to get a little buzz to help me through. I remembered it all.

I have always hated it when people asked me, "If you could change one thing about your life...?"

I always answered, "Dying." It guarantees a few strange looks, but I have never yet felt the need to explain myself.

Rich poked his head around the corner. "But you probably know that a little better than I do."

"Yeah." I forced a smile and shook my head. "I'm going to hop into the shower. Try and wake up a little."

I walked into the bathroom and closed the door. I turned the hot water all the way up and didn't even touch the cold. Immediately, the bathroom started filling up with steam. The mirror became foggy, and my reflection slowly disappeared. I stripped down, threw my clothes into a pile, and stepped in.

As I picked up the soap, I could feel the tears well up. I ran the soap over my body as they started to stream. I scrubbed harder. I wanted to get rid of the memories I could see imprinted on myself, but the harder I washed, the more apparent they became, and the harder I cried.

I leaned my head against the wall and welcomed the scalding water running down my back. The pain was unbearable. I needed to punish myself for thinking about it, for remembering it, but most of all for missing it.

I punched the tile, hard, and started to scream, trying to stop myself from remembering. The more I yelled the worse it got. I started to hit the tile harder. My knuckles split open, and blood fell along the shower wall. The hot water stung along the fresh wounds. I clenched my fists harder. In my ears I could hear a continuous, monotonous beep that started to inflame.

I covered my ears. Blood from my hands poured over my head and face, and I sobbed as I collapsed to the floor, begging for it to stop. The water was burning my skin, but it felt good to take the pain away from where it really hurt. I lowered my head and let the water beat me down, washing the blood from my hair and off my body. I was lost, terrified, and I completely understood how Rich felt. It was a terrible feeling that grew from the pit of my stomach and radiated through every inch of my body. I wanted it to end, but I knew I could do nothing but wait for it to stop.

Rich

Rich's parents were real estate tycoons in Northern Virginia. Mr. and Mrs. Stevens owned office buildings, apartment complexes, and large portions of what little barren land there was all over the D.C. Metro area.

At the age of five, Rich was enrolled in a private school that was famous for shaping young men and women into great leaders. Hanging in the hallways of his parents' house were pictures of young Rich sitting on President Reagan's lap and shaking hands with Bush, Sr. The Stevenses were on their way to becoming the next Rockefellers or Kennedys of America, and they were paving Rich's future for great success.

When he was six years old, his parents flew to Alaska to visit an old college buddy who had made a fortune in oil out there. They never returned.

Rich always said that on the night of the plane crash, he woke up from a deep sleep and immediately knew—his parents were dead.

Rich lived with his only surviving grandmother for the next ten years and started, at a very young age, to learn the family business. He continued on in private schools and met with congressmen, senators, and CEOs of major corporations who all marveled at the promise that he showed.

Old age eventually got the best of his grandmother, and with no legal guardian, he became a ward of the state. He decided, with the advice of a financial advisor, to sell off all of his father's properties, and transferred the profits into interest baring accounts and low yield stocks—options that would continue to show gains in the future. The money that his money earned was put into a trust fund that would become his on his 18th birthday, handsomely setting Rich up for life.

He graduated from public school and then used some of the money to travel around the world. He went to Carnival in Rio, Oktoberfest in Germany; he ran with the bulls in Pamplona, lost his virginity to a prostitute named Jayme in Amsterdam, and backpacked through Thailand.

After two years of traveling, he returned to Virginia, bought a small condo, and spent his days calling the people who managed his money, just so he would have someone to talk to. He decided he needed to do something in order to pass the time, meet some people, and end the awful monotony of his days so he got a job working in a coffee shop.

One day, he was at work, scribbling something on a napkin when Chris and I walked in. He covered it up when we came to the counter.

"I take it you don't like it," Chris said, pointing to the napkin.

"Why would you say that?" he asked.

"If it was good, why would you not want to show it off?" I asked.

He pulled it out and turned it around for us to read.

"You guys want your usual?"

We nodded while scanning the poem.

The pains I live with,
The pains I hold true,
All develop from a source,
All come from a center.

The visions I see while asleep,
The illusions I see while awake,
Are all branched from the same root,
All burning from the same spark.

Demons that torture,
Devils that beat,
Are in my life,
And don't want to leave.

I beg to be free,
I try to escape their grasp,
They hold on tight,
And drag me back in life.

You gave them to me,
And one day I will be free,
Look back and thank them,
And move on in my quest.

Chris and I looked at each other and nodded approvingly.

"It's Rich, right?" Chris asked.

"Yeah," he said as he put two coffees down in front of us. "Chris and Neal, right?"

"Yeah," I said. "What do you call that?"

"Still Alive," he said. "It's $4.50."

We pulled the money out and paid him.

"Who's it too?" Chris asked.

Rich looked at us and shook his head. "Whoever runs the show we call life."

That night the three of us drove to Philly to grab a cheesesteak at 2:30 in the morning. Rich had to open the shop the next morning, and we ended up staying with him all day. We drank coffee, wrote, and talked about life. After that the three of us were inseparable and were usually found at either the diner or the coffee shop.

The twosome had become a threesome. Our saga continued on with a new character and new paths to explore.

IX.

I fell asleep after my shower. Rich had seen the cuts on my knuckles and let me use his room. He wanted to ask, but he knew I wouldn't explain.

It was a much-needed five hours of rest, and I awoke feeling refreshed. My hand was throbbing, but it was nothing more than a slight reminder. I put some pressure on my knuckles to subside the pain.

When I walked into the living room, I felt like I had walked into a new place. Rich, Chris, and Johnson had gone out while I was asleep and picked up all new furnishings. The new leather couch, armchair, and matching ottoman, along with a few colorful throw rugs, gave the formerly drab room a new life. A bag of new sheets for the bed sat on the couch.

"What's up, Neal?" Rich said, sipping on coffee and smoking a cigarette. "How was your nap?"

"Good," I said, giving him a confused look. I pointed at the cigarette in his hand. "You don't smoke."

"Yeah." He took another sip of coffee. "Johnson's idea, said I might want something to help ease the withdrawals."

I looked at Johnson. "Big tobacco thanks you."

"I do it for the tobacco farmers, hurt by all the new health conscious consumers who are quitting," he joked. "Many of whom live right here in Virginia."

"That, and with Rich smoking in here, we don't feel as guilty smoking in here anymore," Chris said while flipping through the TV channels.

I sat down on the couch and took a look around. "The place looks good."

"Thanks," Rich said, taking a drag.

"How do you like it?" I asked.

He shrugged. "It's different, but I'll get used to it."

"Sort of like your life," Johnson said.

Rich nodded. His life was in the midst of receiving the same facelift as his apartment. I hoped that it would be as successful of an endeavor.

Chris turned off the TV and leaned back on the couch. He looked over and noticed my hand.

"Jesus, Neal, what the fuck happened to your hand?"

I looked up at Rich who just shrugged. He had no idea what was going on in the bathroom, and I certainly couldn't explain what had happened and make it sound sane.

"Neal hit me," I said with a smile, giving Chris a sly look out of the corner of my eye.

"That guy's a bastard," Chris said. "He hit me and Johnson yesterday."

"Fucking out of control," I said.

I pulled out a cigarette and lit it. Inhaling the smoke I felt almost at peace with everything in the world. For a moment.

"What are we doing tonight?" I asked.

Rich jumped right in.

"Mmm," he said, his mouth full of coffee. "Tonight this band, Clemency Bay, is playing at this bar. I want to check them out."

"What kind of music?" Johnson asked.

"They're an earthy, edgy, aggressive folk rock band," he said.

Chris, Johnson, and I looked at each other. Rich had always been more into punk, and the rest of us didn't know how we felt about "aggressive folk rock." Rich saw the look of doubt on our faces and sighed.

"The lead singer is this really hot chick," he admitted, his cheeks turning a slight twinge of pink.

"Oh, all right," I said after hearing this simplest of explanations. "I'm down."

"Me too," Chris said quickly.

"What time?" Johnson asked.

"Nine o'clock," Rich said as he walked into the kitchen to get more coffee. Chris started to ask a question but Rich cut him off. "And yes, a lot of hot girls go to see them."

When we got to the bar, Clemency Bay was already playing. Rich was true to his word—the lead singer was incredible, and the place was packed with hot girls. I looked around, hoping that the next hot vehicle that passed would hit me.

"We need a round?" Chris shouted over the music.

All of us nodded, and Chris shoved his way through the crowd to the bar.

"You going to be okay here?" I asked Rich, leaning in and yelling loud enough to be heard.

"I was a drug addict, not an alcoholic," he said. "Besides, my libido is through the fucking roof."

I understood. When I quit using, the desire to have sex increased immensely. I had no idea how long it had been since I last had sex, but I knew that I really wanted to again. It was almost like another withdrawal symptom. Suddenly, these activities that many people considered life-affirming became the only thing to look forward to. Then they became a necessity, almost an obsession. I had turned from drug addict to sex addict in a matter of weeks. By the time I realized that I was doing my body another disservice and being equally brazen and dangerous with a new addiction, the drug withdrawals were minimal, and I was exceptionally lucky to be disease free.

Chris came back with the beers and we all greedily took one. Rich guzzled his down in a single gulp and slammed the glass on the table. He looked around the bar and nodded.

"I'm going to get another one," he said. "Then I got to do this solo."

Rich turned and disappeared into the crowd at the bar. I looked to Chris and Johnson. They were savoring the sights and sounds, deciding where they wanted to move in, and discussing strategy for the best way to approach a girl.

I always recommended just going up and saying "Hi," but they insisted that they needed a routine or game or whatever they called it.

"Chris," Johnson said, nodding toward a group of girls. "Be my wing man."

"Let's go. Neal, you want to…" He motioned to the group.

"No, you guys go ahead, I'll be alright." I took a sip of my beer and looked away for a quick second.

Before I had the chance to look back in their direction, they were gone. I watched as they infiltrated the women with handshakes and introductions.

"And he has Kate," I said to myself, shaking my head.

I walked through the crowd, listening to the music. I had been in Nashville for the last few months and I learned that I really don't know music very well. I had pretentious friends that would tell me what was good and what wasn't. What I learned when I was there was what I liked, and what I didn't. Here I thought the band was actually really good. The lead singer sung with passion and flare. She also played a guitar—gracefully but forceful enough to get the crowd moving. Apart from her, the band only consisted of a drummer.

While I stood there watching them play, someone tapped me on the shoulder. Unsure of who would possibly be attempting to get my attention in such a passive way, I turned to see Lance Baylor standing right behind me.

Lance was an old friend of mine. He was tall and slender with short, dark, and slightly curly hair. His rectangle shaped, wire-rimmed glasses sat at the end of the bridge of his hooked nose. It was a rare occasion that he didn't have a t-shirt on with either a witty saying or a Star Wars reference. Today his shirt read: "Proud to be AWESOME."

Lance had worked at the coffee shop before Rich. We used to talk and play chess all day long. Four years ago, he left to join the Air Force, and I hadn't seen him since.

"Holy shit!" I exclaimed, hugging him. "How have you been?"

"Excellent, man, excellent." Lance was the type of guy who was always in a good mood. He always had something nice to say about everyone. If ever there was a time that my mood was less than jovial, I always felt better if I saw him. "How have you been?"

"I've been good," I said.

"You look great," he said, looking me up and down. "Especially since I heard you were dead."

"Yeah," I said nervously, "well, rumors of my death were grossly exaggerated."

"That's good to hear," he said with a grin. "So you're doing well?"

"Yeah, I am," I said, nodding and taking a sip of my beer. "How is the Air Force?"

"It's good, I still love it. You know, I didn't know if this was really you or not. My friend asked me if I knew who you were, and I couldn't believe that a dead man was here." He had a huge smile on his face. "So talk to me, what happened? How did rumors of your death go around?"

"Wait," I said, seeing my opportunity to dodge the question. I had a lot of practice in that field. "Who's your friend that wanted to know who I was?"

Lance cocked his head slightly to the side and smiled at me.

"God, you never change, Neal."

He turned around and motioned for his friend to come over. I tried to see who it was through the crowd. Suddenly, through the parting sea of people, I saw her. She had the cutest button nose and blue eyes that sparkled in the dimly lit bar. She stopped next to Lance and flashed me an incredible smile.

"Meagan, I'd like you to meet Neal Junior," Lance said. "Neal, this is Meagan McGreggor."

"Nice to meet you," she said, extending her hand.

"You can't say that yet," I said, taking her hand and gently shaking it.

She smiled at me again. There was no hint of nervousness in her eyes. She carried herself with an air of self-confidence that I have rarely seen in people. I had been told that I had a healthy amount of self-confidence, but in her presence I questioned why I deserved to be there.

I stared into her eyes and got lost. It was like looking up at the sky on a cool summer night and seeing all of the stars that shine down upon the world. Like realizing that there was more to this universe than just you and being thankful that you were alive. She had amazing eyes.

Even though I knew I wouldn't, I wanted to remember another time this had happened when I met someone. There was no bar set here for me, no standard way of acting. I was flying blind in enemy territory.

"I'm going to the bar, y'all need anything?" Lance asked, knowing that we weren't paying much attention to him.

"I'm good," I said, breaking my gaze and holding up my almost full beer.

"Me too," Meagan said, mouthing something to him that I couldn't see.

"Alright, I'll be back...later." He disappeared from our view.

"Come on," Meagan shouted as she took my hand. "Let's go somewhere quieter."

We walked to a back hallway away from the music and the crowd. I leaned up against a wall, as she stood there slowly swaying. I'm not sure if it was from the alcohol or just a nervous habit, but I found it very sexy.

"You like Clemency Bay?" she asked.

"This is the first time I've heard them," I said, "but I like what I've heard."

"Would you like them if she wasn't so pretty?"

"Yes," I said defensively, even though I knew that probably wasn't the real answer. "I probably wouldn't have come to see them tonight though."

She laughed at my poor attempt at a joke. It was a great laugh. Her entire body came to life. I could do nothing but stand there and grin like an idiot.

"Why did Lance think you were dead?" she asked.

"Oh." She went straight for the hardest question first. I didn't know what to say. "That was a huge misunderstanding."

"What happened?" Her eyes were filled with concern, even though the incident occurred a year ago.

"It's not important," I said, trying my hardest to duck the question without being rude.

"Come on, tell me," she insisted.

"I haven't even told my best friends what happened, and I don't think we're there quite yet," I said.

"Fine." She gave me a pouty look that was insanely cute and almost convinced me to break down and tell her.

"So, what do you do?" I asked, trying to keep the conversation moving.

"God, that was the worst segue I've ever heard in my life." She shook her head.

"Yeah, I'm sorry. I blame the alcohol," I said, holding up my beer. "So, what do you do?"

She laughed. "I'm a nanny. I babysit three kids from eight to six every day."

"Oh, that's cool. I take it you like kids?"

"Some of them," she said with a smile. "The ones I can give back at the end of the day."

I nodded. I couldn't help but agree.

"What about you? What do you do?" she asked.

"Whatever I can to make money," I said. I learned a long time ago that if you tell a girl you're a writer, she immediately thinks, "Broke."

"Oh Jesus. Actor or writer?" she asked, leaving room for a pause.

"Prostitution," I said.

"Really?" she asked. "Is it good work?"

"It's not too bad."

"Do you get dental with that?" She smiled.

"No. The benefits suck, but the work is fun."

She laughed again. I timidly bit my lip and smiled at her.

"Seriously," she said. "What do you do?"

"Writer."

"Really?" She almost seemed excited. "Would I have read anything of yours?"

"Probably not," I said. "Not unless you spend all day finding rare, hard to find copies of small magazines like 'The Subterranean.'"

"You were published in 'The Subterranean?'" she exclaimed, her eyes alive with fervor.

"You know it?" I asked, amazed. Nobody knew what 'The Subterranean' was. It had a single issue many years before. Then they ran out of money when it didn't sell well…or at all.

"Know it?" she said. "I've never heard of it." She smiled at me, and I forced an embarrassed smile back.

"Yeah, that was cute," I said, embarrassed that I fell for her rouse.

I spotted Lance heading toward us. He looked apologetic for interrupting as he walked up.

"Meagan, I need to get out of here," he said.

"Oh, that means I have to go too," she said to me as her smile turned into a pouty little frown. I was disappointed, but I didn't want to appear so.

"Alright." I turned to Lance as nonchalantly as I possibly could. "Lance, it was good to see you. How long are you in town for?"

"I leave tomorrow."

"Oh damn, that sucks. I would love to hang out with you more."

"Well, Meagan usually knows when I'm in town so she can tell you when I'll be back," he said with a smile, winking at me so that Meagan couldn't see.

"But I don't have her number," I said, taking the cue and running with it. "How am I going to…?"

"Guys, this is just pathetic." She pulled a pen out of her purse. "I would expect more from a writer."

"I'm still blaming it on the alcohol," I said with a grin.

"Here is my number, Neal," she said. "Give me a call sometime."

She grabbed my wrist gently and wrote her number on the palm of my hand. Then she leaned in to give me a kiss on the cheek.

"I'll talk to you in, what, two days, or is the standard three now?"

I honestly had no clue. I never subscribed to the standard dating rules. I never even knew if I was going to be in the same city for a week so I just called when I wanted to see the person. I never understood the game playing. Chris was the one that followed the rules of dating to a T.

"She's great, isn't she?" Lance joked.

I was again stuck in a stare with her, lost in the night sky that rested inside of her eyes. I slowly nodded, a mildly drunken smile across my lips.

"Yes. Yes, she is," I agreed.

"Later, Neal," Lance said as the two of them started to walk away. I broke my gaze with Meagan and looked up toward him. "Good to know you're alive."

"Yeah, you too," I called to him. Then I floated back into the bar.

Diary Entry VII:

Dear Jack,
    Try this one on for size:
  The plane begins to shake,
  a child starts to cry,
  the innocent are punished,
  FUCK IT ALL, goodbye.
  I'm stuck in reality,
  or is it all fiction?
  I'm without gravity.
  Man, I can't do this.
  I must've hit my head.
  Burned too many cells.
  Expect so damn much
  only from myself.
  But fuck it
  I can't quit,
  not for you, or you, or you, or you.
  I've done it all,
  been everywhere.
  No one knows me,
  you can't make me fall.
  You mean less to me,

than I do to you.
So say what you will,
I look at you,
and I want to say, "fuck you!"
Get off my back,
leave me alone,
or I'll come and find you,
and kill you in your home.
You don't want that,
even I can see.
So go the fuck away.
So I can kill me.

Don't start with me. Shut the hell up. I don't want to hear your shit right now. You can leave me too. Everybody else in my life leaves me, why don't you just leave me too? Fuck you. Fuck you all. I don't need this shit. I don't need any of you.

Rich Stevens

X.

That night the four of us went to the diner. It was busy for a Thursday so we sat on booth benches that lined the walls waiting to be seated. Miss Claudia had the night off. We were drunk and loud. Our voices could probably be heard throughout the noisy diner.

"How'd you fare tonight?" Chris asked me.

"I did alright," I said, thinking about Meagan. "I'm not complaining. How did you end up?"

"Good. I met this girl, Ruth," he said. "I might have to call her sometime."

Johnson leaned forward to look around Rich at Chris. "You know if you had fucked her tonight you would never call her again."

Chris gave him the finger without looking at him.

"I don't do that," he said in defense of himself.

"Mary, Amanda, Lindsey." Johnson started listing off names.

"Fuck off," Chris said.

I leaned my head against the green wall behind me and stared up at the ceiling. I found myself thinking about things I had never thought of before. I was reminded of letters I had read when I was a kid in high school, letters about white picket fences and green, green grass. The American dream or whatever it was referred to now. Whether it was a pipe dream or an actual possibility, at this moment the thought of the open road seemed less appealing to me. For the first time in my life, I could understand why someone would want to stay put to start something.

"What's up with you, Neal? I've never seen you look like this before," Chris interrupted my musings.

"What the hell are you talking about?" I asked, defensively.

"Oh, you like her," he said, halfway making fun. "Could this be the end of the eternal bachelor, Neal Junior?"

"Could this be the end of the currently breathing Chris Franklyn?" I asked, glaring at him.

"Neal's in love!" he said, as though he were six years old. I could imagine him belting out the lyrics to K-I-S-S-I-N-G in his less than sober state and wanted to put an end to it before it began so I threw my elbow into his chest. He let out a gasp and clutched at the spot where my elbow had landed. The pretty but trashy hostess came up and told us that our table was ready.

"I'm going to roll to the bathroom, I'll meet you guys there," I said as they headed for the table.

I tried to think about other things, but my thoughts kept turning back to Meagan. I couldn't wait to talk to her again. I felt like I was back in high school with a schoolboy crush on the most popular girl. There was no rational explanation for any of what I was thinking. I had spent only a few minutes with her, yet I couldn't stop thinking about her. I looked in the mirror and caught myself smiling. I shook my head. Time would change that, it always did.

I walked out of the bathroom and headed for the table when I heard my name being called from behind me. I turned around and looked for the source of the voice. It was definitely a girl's voice, but I didn't recognize any of the people that I saw.

"Neal!" she called again, this time standing up.

"Oh fuck," I said to myself as I laid eyes on Becky. I was hoping that Chris hadn't seen her yet. He had enough going on in his life right now. Seeing her could send him right back to snorting powder, or maybe even worse.

"Hey," I said, trying to sound happy to see her. "What are you doing here?"

She ran up and gave me a hug despite the fact that I had only met her twice before. I quickly noticed that she didn't have a ring on her finger.

"Me and my girlfriends were out drinking," she said, motioning back to some girls sitting on the bench behind her. "Stopped in to sober up a little. Is Chris here?"

It had just become a bob and weave situation.

"I heard you got engaged," I said, knowing that I may have opened the door to a conversation that I wouldn't win. "Congratulations."

"I heard you were dead," she said bitterly.

"Well, I'm not." I was cringing while trying to smile.

"Well, neither am I," she said, her eyes narrowing.

"Dead?" I asked. "I can see that."

I knew I was being a little bit of an asshole, hoping that she would assume I was making drunken attempts at being funny.

"No," she said, shaking her head and holding up her left hand. "Engaged."

I gave her a sarcastic yet embarrassed, "Oh," then, "Sorry about that."

"Well, learning experiences and all that." She dismissed it with a wave of her hand. "Is Chris here though? I really want to see him."

I froze for a second. I knew he shouldn't see her, and I felt obligated to protect him.

"Becky, look." I searched for the right words. "If you care for Chris at all...I mean, if there is even a shred of respect or love for him in there, please, don't go talk to him."

"What do you mean?"

I could tell that I had annoyed her.

"Look, Chris is always going to love you. That's never going to change." I hoped if I appealed to her sensitive side she would understand. "If you go over there, bad things will happen for him. Please, just leave him alone."

Becky's eyes pierced mine so violently, I had to look away.

"Fuck you, Neal," she said.

I guess she wasn't as understanding as I had hoped.

"Whatever. Fine," she said, anger draping her tone. She didn't attempt to mask her contempt for me at that moment. "I'll leave."

She stormed out the door, and four other girls ran out after her. I turned, walked to the table, and sat down.

"What took you so long?" Johnson asked. "Did you have to rub one out?"

"Did we order already?" I asked, completely passing off Johnson's comment.

"Yeah," Rich said as he stared at the cherry of his cigarette.

I could see that Rich was not with us. Physically he was sitting there, but in an alcohol induced haze that formed a film over his mind's eye, creating a filter between the fiction he created in his head and the reality that rested in the sobriety of the real world. The way he fidgeted in the booth, the way he stared at the red, glowing tip of his constantly shrinking cigarette, I could see that the fiction he had created was centered on another fix. He was not doing well.

"Anyway," said Chris, talking excitedly, not noticing that Rich was growing more annoyed with each passing second. I could almost see the fuse on his temper burning down to its final threads. "It just pisses me off when I know that I could take a girl home, but I don't. It's supposed to make it better when you finally do take her home, but whatever. What's that called again?"

"Pleasure delaying," I said, stirring my coffee and closely watching Rich's eyes.

"Right. It's a fucking load of crap," Chris said boisterously. "Sex is great anytime."

"I hear that!" Johnson said drunkenly while raising his glass in a toast.

"I should have taken her home," Chris repeated, shaking his head. "I could have taken her home."

"Maybe you could have, but you didn't," Rich spat out as the fuse of annoyance finally ran out, and the time bomb that rested in the boroughs of his soul finally went off. "I'm sure we all could have gotten fucking lucky tonight if we had tried a little harder. All we have is a table full of people sitting in the same shitty diner where we have always sat, throwing the same shitty excuses around that we always have."

He paused and took a drag from his cigarette. Nobody spoke for fear of what he would say in response.

"Pleasure delaying," he scoffed. "Fucking pleasure delaying. Yes, pleasure delaying is a load of crap, but not because of what it does or doesn't do for the sex. Does it make it better? Who knows? I've had one night stands that were incredible, and I've been in relationships where the sex was crap the first time, and vice versa."

He clenched his fists, and I could see his entire body tense up. The pain of whatever he was dealing with at that moment crossed his face in a flash of fear and torment.

He went on. "It's a load of crap because it's just an excuse to use when we don't get lucky. None of us is here because we're pleasure delayers. We're here because we didn't get lucky, and it's easier to give a list of excuses than to admit we just don't have what it takes to be wanted by anyone else."

Rich went back to blankly staring at his cigarette as we all stared at him.

"Bad night, buddy?" Johnson asked.

"Yeah," Rich said, stubbing out his cigarette. He looked out the window to a parking lot full of cars. People were sitting in their cars, waiting for the cops to leave the adjacent parking lot before they attempted to drive away safely.

Nobody knew what to say after that so we just sipped our coffee, smoked our cigarettes, and wished that the food would come soon.

"Why are you so quiet, Neal?" Chris asked, hoping to start another conversation.

"I've..." I started, wanting to tell him about Becky, but I knew that he would be upset. I would tell him the next day when we were both sober and able to discuss it like rational adults. "I've just got a lot on my mind."

"Aw," Chris cooed, "Neal's in love."

I threw another elbow into his chest. I knew I was going to regret that one when he found out about Becky.

We left the diner without having said much to each other.

"What are you all doing?" I called as we walked to our cars. Rich walked straight to my car and got in the passenger side.

"I'm going home," Chris said. "I want to sleep in my own bed."

"Yeah, I'm doing the same. I need a good night's sleep," Johnson yelled. "Unfortunately Rich's floor is not as comfortable as my Chrisress."

"Cool. Call us tomorrow," I said as I got into the car and started it up.

I noticed Rich was staring out the window. His eyes were vacant and hollow. A thin veil of perspiration covered his forehead and was running down his cheeks. He had barely touched his food.

"Rough night, huh?" I asked.

"Tell me it gets easier," he said.

"It, it gets easier," I said, trying my best to sound convincing. It had only been a couple of days for Rich. It took me weeks to get through the bulk of my issues. Once the physical addiction subsided, the mental addiction still had a stronghold on me. I didn't want to lie to Rich and give him false hope so I told him honestly, "But not for a long time."

Rich nodded and put his head against the window for the rest of the drive to his house.

Diary Entry VIII:

Dear Jack,

    I miss them more on days like today. I wonder how differently I might have turned out if they were still around. Would I look forward to my dealer bringing his daily little treat? Or would I be interning for some government big wig up on Capitol Hill? Or would I be stuck somewhere in between? You hear of these orphans with abandonment issues, searching for their parents who gave them away when they were very young, searching for a meaning in a meaningless existence. But I can't do that. My parents didn't not want me, they fucking died. I can't find them hiding out on some hippie commune filled with has-beens, and people who are trying too damn hard to be young, and suddenly have closure. I know where they are. They're in the fucking cemetery. I swear, life isn't fair to people with dead parents.

    I saw Claire today. She was looking as stellar as ever. We took a walk around old town and caught up on the past few weeks. God, I can't believe that it had been a month since I had last seen her. Her bright red hair shone like a beacon of hope on the rainy, gloomy day that preceded this entry to you. She was wearing these low cut jeans leaving very little to my overly active imagination. It was a great afternoon. We talked about what we had planned for the next few weeks, where that was going to lead us. I was again mesmerized by everything about her. The sun would peek out from behind a cloud every so often and reflect off of the downy hair that covered her arms. Her green eyes saw into the depths of my soul, and without me telling her she looked inside and knew that I was a user. I could tell by the way that she talked to me. Oh well, she had a date tonight anyway. Some guy named Dylan. I wished her luck and told her not to stay out too early.

I gots to go, Jack, my man's here, and a night of chemical bliss awaits me.

'Til next time,
Rich Stevens

XI.

That night I slept soundly. It was the first solid eight hours of uninterrupted sleep I had gotten since my arrival. The only problem was, I could have slept for nine or ten.

My eight glorious hours were interrupted when the front door was thrown open, slamming into the wall. My eyes shot open but not fast enough. Chris already had me by the shirt. He pulled me off the couch and threw me to the floor. I tried to stand up, but he kicked me in the side, knocking the wind out of me and sending me back to the floor.

"You mother fucker!" he screamed, as he grabbed me by the back of my shirt and threw me into the wall adjacent to the couch. "You meddling piece of shit!"

I slid down the wall, gasping for breath, trying to wake up. Getting my ass kicked wasn't really helping me get my head straight. I was foggy, and my fight or flight responses weren't working as quickly as I needed them to be.

My breath started to come back as I crawled around on the floor. Chris pulled me up again and threw me back into the wall, knocking the breath out of me again. I gasped and clutched my chest as his fist connected with my mouth. I felt the inside of my lip split before I hit the floor again, along with large, dark drops of my own blood.

"I can't believe you did that!" he yelled, kicking me. I cringed, trying to defend myself, curling up into the fetal position to keep my head and ribs covered, but he was kicking too hard. Each kick left me open to another one that had greater impact than the one before it. "Why did you feel the need to get involved in my life?"

Thankfully, Rich came tearing out of his room, still wearing only his boxer shorts. He grabbed Chris and threw him across the room. Chris stumbled back a few feet, nearly falling backwards over the coffee table, but he was able to catch himself and keep his balance.

"What the fuck?" Rich screamed as I struggled to my feet. "This is not how I like to wake up every fucking morning."

"That piece of shit," Chris yelled, lunging for me again, but Rich caught him and pushed him back. "Who do you think you are?"

Finally on my feet, I wiped the blood from my mouth. Everything hurt. I was certain I had cracked a rib or two in the onslaught.

"What the fuck are you talking about?" My sides stung as I talked. I cupped them with my arms for relief.

"What do you think, you asshole? Becky called me." He yelled at me over Rich's defending shoulder. "You self-righteous prick. Why do you want to rule my life?"

I was bending over from the pain. I had feared that this would happen before I had a chance to talk to him. I watched the blood drip from my lip onto the floor, and all of a sudden, I hated him.

I hated him for his arrogance. I hated him for his inability to get over things. I hated him for his attachments to people and things that really didn't matter in our world. I hated him for his inability to see how good of a person he was, how much he had to offer to a world that needed good, honest people. I hated him for allowing himself the ability to become someone who was no longer good, or honest. I hated him for not believing in himself, which made him not believe in any of us as well. I hated him for all of these reasons and so many more.

"Did you want me to just let her talk to you?"

"Fuck yes!" He was trying to push past Rich to get at me, but even in Rich's weakened state he was able to keep Chris back.

"What is your issue? You dumb mother fucker!" I said through the pain. Breathing was difficult, my lip had begun to swell, and my arm felt like he had bruised the bone. "Do you just like to torture yourself? You are such an emotional sadist."

"Fuck you, Neal!"

"No, fuck you, Chris. Now I know, next time I'll let her talk to you. So when she breaks your heart again..." I said the words with all of the malice and contempt I had for the two of them. "...just like the time before and the time before that...then you can hate yourself for what happened and you can turn back into a junkie. Only this time I won't be around. Don't think you can call me up and cry away another fucking breakfast with me."

"What?" Rich looked at me, shocked, then back at Chris.

"Fuck you, Neal," Chris said loudly. "Fuck you."

"Yeah, that's right, Rich," I said, raising my arms as I let loose with the truth. "You've been clean longer than Chris has. You've been clean for what, five days? Chris's only on day three."

Chris lunged at me again. Rich grabbed him and threw him to the floor, but he was able to jump back up quickly and rush me. Rich grabbed him from behind, restraining his left arm while he swung at me wildly with his right, narrowly missing my face.

"I will fucking kill you," he screamed trying to break free of Rich's grasp.

"I've died before," I said calmly, coldly. "I can do it again."

"I wish you'd have fucking stayed that way," he said with as little emotion in his voice as possible.

"Whoa," Rich said, pulling back on Chris's arm and wrapping both arms around his chest to hold him back. "Don't say anything you won't be able to take back."

Chris stared at me. He wasn't going to apologize for what he had said. I shook my head.

"I'm out of here," I said. "One day you'll thank me."

"Fuck you, Neal," he said, watching me as I walked by. "I'll never thank you for this."

I turned and punched him across the face in the same place I'd hit him two days earlier. His body went limp, and Rich dropped him to the ground. Now the third time I had hit someone in my life.

"You're ungrateful. An ingrate," I said, and I walked out the door.

I heard the door slam shut behind me as I stormed down the stairs and into the parking lot. There, I let out a primal rage, blood spewing from my mouth and dripping onto my shirt, squirting randomly on the parked cars around me. I punched and kicked at the metal community mailbox, somehow managing to bend its support legs.

"Hey!" a voice called out behind me.

I turned to see an old, blue-haired woman in her long, cotton, floral nightgown, standing on her upstairs balcony staring down at me.

"What?" I bellowed from my place on the ground, screaming at the judgmental hag that was imposing herself at a time when I didn't need or want anyone's opinion of who I was or what I was doing.

"You can't do that!" She screamed down at me with the voice of a person who had spent too many years of her life smoking. "It's a federal offense."

"Fuck off, bitch," I said, just loud enough for her to hear. I stalked off to my car, got in and slammed the door.

Reversing out of the parking spot, I came within inches of the car parked directly behind mine before hitting the brakes. I shifted into first gear and sped out of the parking lot, swerving and skidding the whole way. I knew I was out of control, but I didn't care.

Thoughts bounced around in my head. Thoughts of leaving and never coming back, getting in my car and driving so very far away. Thoughts of a nature so dark I swore, long ago, that I would never think them again.

Thoughts of dying, not of suicide, just of dying, so that Chris could feel like shit and realize what he had done.

I was doing 40mph as I turned left around a blind corner, cursing Chris's name the entire time. Suddenly, I found myself face to face with a white semi truck that was blowing its horn at me. I spun the wheel sharply to the right, narrowly missing the truck, but jumping the curb and heading straight for a stand of trees. Quickly turning the wheel left, I slammed on the brakes and fishtailed. Somehow I ended up facing the street so I rolled back over the curb and parked the car.

My heart was pounding, and I was covered in sweat. As I turned the car's ignition off, I noticed that my hands were shaking violently. I slowly got out of the car and closed my door. I put my head face down on the roof and let the tears slowly fall onto the white chipped paint.

The driver of the truck got out and ran over to me, shouting, "Son, are you okay?"

I lifted my hand to wave at him, then turned and spit some blood to the ground. I wiped any that was left behind from my lips and rubbed my hand onto my already bloody shirt.

"Do you need an ambulance?" he asked.

I shook my head. "I could use a cigarette though."

He pulled one out and handed it to me. I grabbed the zippo out of my pocket and smiled slightly as the telltale ping rang through the air when I opened it. I lit the cigarette and leaned back against the car. My head was swimming. I felt dizzy and shocked. Anger still surged through my blood, but a feeling of just being happy to be alive slowly began to take over. Then I thought about Meagan.

"You gonna be okay, son?"

"Yeah," I said with a vacant smile. "I'm going to call Meagan."

"You do that," he said nervously, backing slowly away. "I have to go."

"Later." I waved. "Thanks for the cigarette."

"No problem," he said, then turned and ran back to his truck, quickly jumping in and pulling away.

I grabbed my phone out of my pocket. I didn't know why, but I knew that I wanted to talk to Meagan at that moment. After three rings, she picked up.

"Hello?" Her voice rang through the phone. Hearing it made me smile, and my lip split open a little wider.

"Hi Meagan," I said, wiping some fresh blood from my lips. "It's Neal."

I explained the situation to her. She said that she couldn't meet up with me just yet, but she would call me once she got off work. She also gave me Lance's number so I could talk to him before he went back to the Air Force. Lance and I talked for a while and agreed to meet at the coffee shop where he and Rich used to work.

He was already there when I arrived, sitting at a table sipping on a coffee and reading a magazine that looked like it was over a year old. I tapped him on the shoulder.

When he turned around, a shocked expression crossed his face. "Hey Buddy! You look like shit."

I had to agree with him. Blood covered my shirt, my lip had swollen up to the size of a marble, I could barely breathe without cringing, and I had trouble standing up straight. I hadn't showered yet, my body was covered in sweat, and I was still shaking from my near miss accident.

"Yeah," I said, wincing. Talking sent a sharp pain through my side. "I got my ass kicked."

"Yeah, Meagan told me what happened."

Lance stood up walked with me over to one of the couches on the opposite side of the room.

"You want some coffee?" he asked.

I nodded and felt my lip.

"Don't touch it, it'll make it worse," he scolded.

"Thanks, Mom."

He shook his head and walked away to get my coffee. "No problem, son."

I looked around the coffee shop, taking in all the people that were hanging out. A few were working on homework or office assignments. Others appeared to be avoiding work. It felt like the entire quilted fabric of human existence was present in this singular spot, and I could see that almost everyone was struggling with the same issues. In their own unique way, they were all trying to find themselves, and not one looked successful. Everyone had a sadness in his eyes, hidden beneath the guise of what I could only describe as an optimism that tomorrow would bring a slightly better day.

Lance came back with the coffee and a small bag of ice.

"The guy behind the counter thought you might want this."

I took it and waved my thanks to the red-haired kid behind the counter. Lance sat down and pulled out a chess game from beneath the table. I looked around and noticed that all of the tables had board games under them. Chess, Backgammon, Mah-jongg.

"How long has it been?" he asked.

"A while," I said, and my smile split my lip open again causing a small amount of pain to coarse through my head.

Lance took my hand with the ice in it and guided it to the swollen welt on my lip.

"This way I won't have to listen to you talk too much," he said with a crooked grin.

When Lance had worked at the coffee shop, he and I would play chess for hours. We had completely different styles of playing. I always went for the quick kill whereas he liked to take out all of my men before going for the king. He loved to play me while I was writing because I never paid attention to the game, and he could take me for six games in a row without even having to think.

We set up the board and started to play. Immediately our different styles became apparent. I aggressively moved to the front lines, while he slowly began to build up a strategic defense, planning many moves in advance.

"So, where have you been since..." He looked up at me. "You know."

"Everywhere," I said, staring down at the board with hopes of avoiding this conversation. "I couldn't be here so I was everywhere else."

"Where was your favorite?"

I looked up. I wasn't expecting that question, but now that it had been posed I realized that I had no idea.

"Depends," I said after a second. "Are we talking about a single moment? Or as a whole, or the people, or what?"

"Everything," he said as he moved a piece on the chessboard.

I sat back and stared at the ceiling for a moment, then leaned forward.

"As far as people go, I liked Tennessee. I met some really cool people in Nashville. Really friendly. Great music too." I thought about some of the friends I had made there. That town was filled with dreamers, passionate people who wanted something great for their lives.

"You still friends with any of them?" Lance asked.

"On occasion I hear from some of them," I said, thinking about how I needed to call some of them. "Not as often as I would like."

"What about the best city?"

"The coolest city was Minneapolis/St. Paul," I said. "When the sun reflects off the lakes...oh my God, it could make a non-believer believe, even if only for a minute. In fact, it almost did."

Lance smiled. He knew about my religious beliefs, or lack thereof, but he himself was a firm believer in God and

Jesus. He had often tried to convert me to follow the path of redemption, but I always politely declined.

"The best all around was Tucson," I said. "I fell in love with that place. I almost didn't come back. Hiking through the canyons was nothing short of inspiring."

Lance took his turn and looked back up at me.

"The single greatest moment, however, was in Texas, I-20. Mile post 64." I looked down at the board and moved.

"Why there?"

"Because you own the world there. Every direction you look, there's nothing but highway and desert." I closed my eyes and thought about my short time there. It was a barren wasteland, but it was perfect. It taught me that everyone on this world has a purpose and a destiny. "I know it sounds crappy, but for ten minutes, I was the only one around, all the way to the horizon in every direction. I was at the top of the world, the only person on it. It was mine."

"What happened?"

I smiled as I took my turn.

"A truck came by and took away my solitude," I said, "so I left. But for those ten minutes, it was flawless."

Lance stared at the board and moved again. "Why did you leave Tucson if you loved it so much?"

"A friend of mine needed me to come back," I said, taking my turn.

"You really care about your friends that much?" he asked.

"Let me ask you this," I said, cringing at the idea of actually answering a question with another question.

"Who is richer—the man who has the most expensive funeral or the man who has the most people come to his funeral?"

Lance nodded then moved.

"I want to be very rich when I die," I said, making my final move. "Checkmate."

Lance stared at the board in shock. "I let you win."

"I'm glad," I said. "I've had a shitty day, and it's not even noon."

Diary Entry IX:

Dear Jack,

I can't think. It's so hard to find the shit to complete a story or even a fucking poem. It's all electrical impulses that aren't reaching their destination. I feel like I am here but I'm dead. I just can't concentrate on anything.

Anyway, I'm out.

Rich Stevens

XII.

Lance let me shower at his house and loaned me some clean clothes. He was a good four inches taller than me so everything was much too big for me. The shirtsleeves hung well past my hands so I had to keep pulling them up to my wrists in order to use my hands to pull up the pair of jeans that kept falling halfway to the ground before I could pull them back up.

When I walked out of the bathroom, Lance couldn't help but laugh at me.

"That's a good look for you," he said.

"Shut the hell up. I'm short."

We walked into the kitchen, and he tossed me a soda.

"Feel better?" he asked as we sat down at the table.

"No, not really," I admitted. I felt cleaner, but I still felt like shit. My lip wasn't as swollen, but it still stung whenever I would tongue the cut. I began to wonder if Chris had ample reason to do what he did. Would I have reacted the same way if I had ever understood what love was? Did I actually want to know what love was like if it could make people act like that?

Lance reached into his pocket, pulled out a penny, and flicked it to me.

"Was his reason good enough?" I asked, putting the penny in my pocket.

"If he loves her and wants to be with her then, yes, it was."

"I just wanted to protect him."

"He doesn't see it that way," Lance replied. "He probably sees it as you keeping him from the one thing in this world that he has ever loved."

"She's bad for him," I said.

"It's not your place to decide."

I ran my tongue over my lip where the cut was. Mild pain radiated around the area. I knew Lance was right. I had made a decision for Chris's life based on what I thought was good for him, not based on what he would want. I hadn't done that since the suicide attempt years ago. At the time, he had needed me to be there running things, but not anymore. He had been making all of his own life decisions for quite some time now. I couldn't even remember the last time Chris had actually asked for my advice on anything. He didn't need me anymore. Suddenly I realized why he was so mad at me.

"Fuck," I said softly as my phone started to ring. "Yeah?" I answered without looking.

"Neal, it's Meagan," her voice danced through the phone, instantaneously making me feel a little better. I even got the so-called butterflies in my stomach that I had heard about but had never experienced before. The feeling was odd and new. I was nervous but eager to talk to her. I couldn't hide the smile on my face as the butterflies flittered around my stomach, which felt like it was about to burst.

"Hey," I said, trying not to sound as excited as I was to hear her voice. "What are you up to?"

"Just got off work. Where are you?" she asked.

"Lance's."

"Alright, I'll be there in a minute."

"See you then." I hung up and felt like I might pass out from holding in all of the emotions flooding my body.

I'm certain a goofy smile was plastered across my face. Lance knew before I looked at him.

"Meagan's coming over?" he asked slyly.

"Is that cool?"

"Yeah," he said, physically waving the question away with his hand. "She was coming over anyway to help me load up my Jeep."

"When do you leave?"

"About an hour."

We sat in silence for a minute. Lance had something on his mind, but it was obvious he didn't want to talk about it. I was in the same predicament. Something had entered my mind the night before, but I feared the answer.

"Neal, have you ever been in love?" he finally asked, breaking the silence.

"No. I have felt anger, hatred, I know what it is to love a family member or a friend, but I've never been in love." I was a bit confused by his question. "Why?"

Lance took a sip from his soda as he nervously looked me over.

"Because Meagan will do it to you. She's a great girl. She's fun, intelligent, a smart ass. She'll keep you on your toes," he said solemnly. A slight hint of sadness was hidden in his eyes. Apparently there was more to the Meagan/ Lance story than just good friends. "She will break down any walls you have. You'll be head over heels."

"Happened to you?"

"Yeah," he said. For the first time ever, I heard a sadness in his voice that seemed so very out of place. It's like when you see the beautiful girl, and she has a horse's laugh. It was off-putting and uncomfortable. "But I don't want you to think that I'm asking you not to go for her."

"I don't think I understand."

"You don't know what a girl can do to you," he said. "I've always idolized you, Neal. I always wanted to do what you do. Picking up and leaving, seeing the world, living life."

"You're living life, man," I said. "You get to see the world. You have a bevy of stories. I'm proud of you and all that you have accomplished."

"Alright," he paused, searching for the words. He lightly chewed on the inside of his lip—a sign he was stuck in deep thought. I used to watch him do the same thing during chess matches while he plotted out my demise.

"You don't live life, you stop time," he said after a moment. "The first time you left, deciding when and where to go, you checked your timepiece. It read 'now' and 'there,' letting you know the time was right. The moment you crossed city lines all of our timepieces stopped and didn't start again until you looked down at yours and it told you that it was time to return. Remember the line of that song that goes 'time grabs you by the wrist, directs you where to go?' Well, you grab time by the wrist and tell it where you will go. Fate may control everybody else's destiny, but you, you control the destiny of fate. You're the one who sinks the nine on the break. Draws the ace to complete the straight. You are the impossible man. You are who everybody at that coffee shop wanted to be, and you knew it. But somehow you continued to look up to and admire each of us, as we did to you."

I was in awe. I wasn't used to receiving praise, and even though my ego grew with each word, I became equally humbled by them.

"I guess that I'm saying," he continued, "don't change. If you fall in love, bring whoever she is up to you, don't fall from the pedestal that so many of us have placed you on. We need you to stay who you are. The world needs you."

I didn't know what to say. I was, admittedly, a little misty. I had to admire him for being able to tell me that, hell, my parents could never tell me that. All I could do was reach out my hand. He took it and we shook. I nodded my speechless "thank you."

The front door slowly opened and Meagan came through. She walked into the kitchen in the midst of our passionate handshake.

"Aw," she said, bringing her two index fingers together. "Are you two sharing a moment?"

Meagan and I helped Lance pack up his gear and waved him off as he headed back to the Air Force.

"What now?" I asked.

She looked at me with a sly smile. "How are you feeling?"

"I'm still sore, but I'll survive."

"Good," she said, taking me by the hand and leading me to her car. She opened the passenger door, I got in, and she went around and got in her side. She pulled a quarter out of her pocket and handed it to me. "Heads is right, tails is left."

That night, on what could be considered the first real date that I had ever really had, we flipped our way through Northern Virginia, D.C., and southern Maryland. Every street we passed, we flipped a coin to determine whether we were turning or staying straight. We hit back roads and dead ends where we had to turn around. There were neighborhoods that we went through slowly, enjoying the basic joy of watching people spending the afternoon with their families after a hard day of work. Then there were the other neighborhoods that we sped through, attempting to get out of them as quickly as possible. We ended up on highways and would drive at the amazingly slow pace that only D.C. area traffic allows, taking in the views that were sprawled out on both sides, guided by a force greater than the two of us. The decision on where to go and what road to turn on was controlled by the small, silver coin that was being tossed in the air with the faith that it knew what was right for the two of us at every moment. Although this could go without being said, I am still inclined to say—it was an amazing and glorious night.

While we drove, I caught Meagan up on the entire story. I told her about Rich and his struggle with addiction. I told her about Chris and Rich's falling out. I explained how Johnson and I weren't very close anymore, all because of a girl that I knew for a very short period of time in the grand scheme of eternity. I told her that Chris was probably my best friend and that I found myself waking up with him kicking my ass. She listened and seemed to honestly care about what I was saying and who I was talking about. As the sun was setting we stopped off in Old Town Alexandria by the Potomac River to eat and watch the boats coast by the dock.

After we finished our subs from a local sandwich shop and our rousing game of trash can basketball, Meagan turned to me. "There is something I've been wondering."

"What's that?"

"You said that you took dictation for Rich the other day," she said.

"Yeah."

"But, this man, who couldn't hold a pen, was able to pull Chris away from you when he was trying to kill you," she said with a hint of confusion.

"Oh, well, I wasn't taking dictation for him because he didn't have the strength to hold the pen." I lifted my hand and started shaking it, simulating a withdrawal. "Ever try to write when your hand was doing this?"

She nodded in understanding.

"How long have you been clean?" she asked, her voice filled with a level of sincerity and care that I didn't know people could have for someone they had known for less than 24 hours.

"Why do you think that I used to be dirty?" I asked, slyly peering at her through the corner of my eye.

"Two of your friends are dealing with addiction, and you know what a withdrawal is like. It wasn't a hard puzzle to put together."

I turned away and watched the water drift by the pier. The moon was out early that day. The reflection shone on the water's surface and rippled as boats slowly made their way, enjoying the brisk evening.

The sky was full of oranges, purples, reds, dark blues. In the center of it all hung a huge white moon. I glanced up, wondering how so much time had passed since I had last done anything. It had been a long time, but I still missed it every once in a while. They say there are certain people you never get over. I wondered if, since I had never been addicted to a person, drugs were the one who got away for me. I hoped that there would be a time that I would never think about them again. I wished that even the slight urges that I had on occasion would go away. Maybe it is like the urge to call an ex at two in the morning when you're feeling vulnerable.

"Two years, three months."

"Two years, three months," she repeated. "Isn't that about the time..."

"Two years, three months." I cut her off, snapping my head around, looking at her, annoyed.

"Okay," she said. She could obviously tell that the subject upset me. She lightly put her hand around the back of my neck and gently pulled my head to her shoulder, putting her arm around me.

For a moment I was angry, then with that simple touch, all anger was gone. I closed my eyes as she softly stroked my head.

"What are you going to do when they don't need you here anymore?" she asked.

I opened my eyes. I hadn't thought about that. For a second I was stressed, but she continued to stroke my head, and I calmed down almost immediately.

"I don't know, I haven't really thought about that. I might go back to Tennessee, or maybe Arizona, or somewhere completely new," I said in my state of absolute relaxation. "You want to come?"

She stopped rubbing my head.

"What?" she asked, stunned.

"Do you want to come?" I repeated, lifting my head from her shoulder.

"Neal, I don't think that I should travel across the country with you."

I shrugged. "Okay."

"Why would you want me to?" she asked. Her voice was still filled with surprise.

"Look." I wanted to explain this the best that I could. "Rich, Chris, and Johnson are the only ones that I've ever asked to leave here with me, and I asked all of them within the first three days of knowing them. At the moment that just passed, it felt right to ask you. If you don't want to, it's okay, but if you do, I'm always looking for someone to come with me."

Meagan looked me in the eye, nervously. She was trying to assess the seriousness of the query. I could tell that the question had scared her, and rightfully so. It wasn't every day that the guy you met the day before invites you on a cross-country road trip with him. I had to smile as she searched for the words that sat somewhere on her tongue but couldn't make it out of the gate.

"Forget I asked," I said. "It's not for everybody."

"I've never been away from here," she said.

"I'm sorry," I said as I reached into my pocket and pulled out my cigarettes.

"Why me?"

"Well, you're sweet, you're funny, you're easy to talk to. You're also a hell of a lot better looking than anyone else I've ever asked, and that could boost my appeal."

She smiled.

"The main reason, the deciding factor, is that you're a friend of Lance's, which means you're decent, honest, and caring, all things I need when I'm on the road."

"Will you give me time to think about it?" she asked.

"No," I said coldly.

Her eyes shot around wildly. "That's not fair."

I put my hand on her shoulder. "Hey, I'm kidding. Take all the time you need."

She pulled her shoulder away, and made a mock angry face. "I hate you," she mouthed.

"By all the time you need," I continued, "I mean until I'm getting ready to leave again."

Then she pulled my head back onto her shoulder and continued to run her hand through my hair while we watched the color fade from the sky and allowed the darkness of night take over.

"How do you do it?" she asked.

"What?" I asked, back in my comatose state.

"If another guy asked me to move across the country with him, the day after I met him, I would be calling a cab right now," she said. "But I'm still here, with you, and seriously wondering what would happen if I say yes."

I sat back up and looked at her.

"Because you realize that I'm just kind of a, I hate to say this, but a free spirit," I explained. "I have the capacity to get up and leave at any given moment. I just move from place to place trying to find my next great story, and you know I'm inviting you to be part of a story that could be great."

"How could it be great?" she asked.

"Alright," I said. "I'm tired of talking."

"What does that..." she started to ask, but I broke her off.

I pulled her face in close to mine and placed my lips against hers. At first there was a slight resistance, but it ended almost immediately as she reached her hand around and placed it on the back of my neck. Her lips were soft, and only made me want to never stop kissing her. Her tongue was firm but tender. She tasted sweet, like ripe tropical fruits, from an area of the world that I hadn't been to yet. I pulled her in closer, and she reciprocated by tightening her embrace.

My head began to swim, and suddenly I started to break out in a light sweat. I tried to pull back, but she only held me tighter. The moment was lasting forever, but at the same time not nearly long enough. A lifetime could have been defined in that instant, and all of the beauty in the world became abundantly apparent to me.

After a while, she pulled away and smiled.

"You okay?" she asked.

I looked at her with a confused look. That was not the remarkably memorable statement that one would expect after the greatest first kiss in history.

"Yeah," I said. "Why?"

"It felt like it bothered you," she said.

I smiled and lightly ran my hand along her cheek, tucking a few strands of loose hair behind her ear.

"Not in any way it ever has before."

Diary Entry X:

Dear Jack,

    I just got word, Neal's Dead. I have to go shoot up now.

    Rich Stevens

XIII.

The next morning Meagan dropped me off at my car. I kissed her goodbye and promised to call her later that night. I wasn't sure if I should go back to Rich's, but I didn't have much of a choice as I had nowhere else to go. I hoped that Chris wasn't there. I did not want to see him.

Driving to Rich's felt like walking the last mile. I was hoping for a pardon from the governor, find Rich alone, but I feared no reprieve and expected Chris to be waiting for me. All of the pain that had subsided during the night became exceptionally noticeable the closer I got to Rich's apartment.

When I arrived I could feel my heart pounding in my ears. I slowly opened the door and snuck in, attempting to be as quiet as possible. Cautiously, I came around the corner. I could see someone's feet resting on the coffee table. Preparing myself for the worst I walked into the living room to find only Johnson sitting there.

He looked up at me. "Hey," he said.

"Hey," I said even more tense now. I began to fear an ambush.

Johnson put his notebook down on the couch and stood up. He stretched his fingers, cracked his knuckles.

"How ya doin'?" he asked.

"As well as can be expected." I was aware of everything going on at that moment. The toilet in the bathroom was running, the faucet in the kitchen was dripping, and the ice machine dropped a load of ice. I couldn't hear anyone else though.

Johnson laughed at me.

"Don't worry," he said. "Chris isn't here."

"Where's Rich?" I asked, still apprehensive about the situation.

"With Chris," he said.

Suddenly I realized that Johnson was no danger. He wasn't acting threatening or bitter the way he had been since we all came back. There was a soothing nature to his demeanor. It almost seemed like he was trying to reach out, for the first time in years, so I relaxed. A long sigh left my mouth.

"Feel better?" he asked.

"Much," I said, relieved.

"You still look like shit," he said.

"And to believe I feel worse than that. He got me a few times in the ribs—that still kind of stings when I breathe."

"Taking a size ten to the rib cage multiple times will definitely do that to a person," he said with a smile.

I chuckled, and a slight pain shot through my side. It felt like Johnson and I were friends again, and I wasn't sure how to react.

"Johnson," I said, motioning my hands between us. "Are we...? I mean, are you and I...?"

My voice trailed off as Johnson stood and patted me lightly on the shoulder. He bent over to pick up his notebook and started toward the door.

"Come on," he said. "We need to talk."

Johnson drove me to the battlefield. We got out of the car, and he popped his trunk. He pulled out a Frisbee, and together we walked through the fields to a flat area with picnic tables that had been enclosed by a line of trees.

We threw our notebooks down on a picnic table, and I ran out a few yards as he tossed the Frisbee to me. The cool winter air stung my face, and my breath hung visibly in the air in front of me as the Frisbee whipped through the sky. I reached out to grab it and the hard plastic stung my cold hands. I quickly shook it off and threw it back to him with a quick flick of the wrist. It had been a while since I had last thrown a Frisbee, but it felt good to toss one again.

Years before, the four of us would come to the battlefield and throw the Frisbee around for hours. We would get into two-on-two matches of ultimate and play until one of us was puking or passed out, which due to the amount we smoked, how dehydrated we let ourselves get, and the amount of drugs we all took, could happen rather quickly.

Memories flooded back as Johnson and I tossed the Frisbee back and forth. The warm spring days where the only thing that mattered was who came down with that flying disc. Everything else in the world seemed so extremely trivial. The cool winter nights where we played until steam would rise off our heads, drifting upward into the night sky, disappearing, like all of our problems would as long as we continued to throw the Frisbee back and forth. We found that there was something cathartic about the simple and easy act of tossing that Frisbee back and forth, and we used it as therapy, just how Johnson and I were at that moment.

We didn't say a word for an hour other than the occasional "go long" or "nice catch." Soon we both had smiles on our faces and Johnson knew that it was safe to talk.

"I'm not mad at you," he said, throwing the Frisbee to me.

"What?" I asked as I caught it.

"I'm not mad at you," he said again.

I walked up to him and handed him the Frisbee. "I'm glad."

"Come on," he said, with a wave of the disc, motioning me to come with him as he started walking to the table.

We sat down on the tabletop with our feet resting on the benches. He picked up his notebook and flipped through the pages. His eyes quickly scanned each line, searching for something that would explain his anger toward me. He stopped and slid it over to me.

7 a.m., I'm awake

I look at your face

and wonder what you're dreaming.

Do you want a better life?
A life that I can't give you?
I tried to be
someone I'm not,
just to be with you.
And you flow through me,
my thoughts and my heart.
Sadness sweeps over my body,
for what I know is true.
I see that this is over,
I admit I'm afraid though
'cause I don't want to hurt you.
I wish I never was so proud,
wish you never were so sweet
wish I could give you
anything you wanted,
unless of course, that's me.
Who I am crept up on me,
And won't tiptoe back into the shadows.
I don't want to hurt you
so we must be through.
Even though I love you,
our love has to conclude.
So dream about a better life
and picture me not in it.
Because you will always flow through me
    and I will never flow through you.
    I looked up at him. He was staring at the table.
    "I wrote that the day I heard you died," he said,
looking up from the table and out toward the horizon. He

didn't look at me. I think that if he had looked at me he would have broken down. "It hit me like a fucking ton of bricks. I had become an asshole, and I realized that I wasn't good enough for Kate. She deserved someone that wouldn't have done what I did to you. When she got home that night I handed that to her. She didn't say a word, she hugged me, kissed me on the cheek, then walked into the room while I left."

I wasn't sure if I should say anything. He hit a pause that felt like he was searching for the words, and I didn't want to ruin his train of thought.

"I came back down and moved in with my dad," he continued. "I thought about all the time that we had spent together, as you slowly became a bigger addict, and how I begged you to stop, how much I didn't want to see you in the position you were in. I wondered if there was anything that I could have done to stop you earlier."

It was true. Johnson was right by my side as I slid down the slope of recreational user to full-blown addict. He would tell me to stop, not to buy any more, not to go out because I would use, but I never listened. The only thing that I cared about was scoring. I needed it, the way that Rich needed it, the way that Chris needed it. I was always envious of Johnson for never starting, but he was always the strong one out of us. He had his own demons that he had to deal with, and he always realized that he didn't have room in his life for another vice that could hold him back.

I wouldn't have traded lives with Johnson for anything. Everything that gave him the strength to say no to drugs were things that I probably couldn't have dealt with at all. His strength came from a series of events that a lesser person would have crumbled from. It was because of his resilience that I admired him, and part of me wished that I had his strength.

"Then I heard that you hadn't died, and it pissed me off that I had come to such a huge realization when I heard that you had," he said, shaking his head, the idiocy of his logic bewildering him. "So I blamed you for my break up with Kate. I didn't want to believe that I had been an asshole, or rather that I had become one. I convinced myself that you made me believe that, that your death was an elaborate way to break us up."

He paused and looked me in the eye. I could see the friend that I used to know and love. The man that I considered a brother, the person who had been there for me through so many ups and downs in life. In those eyes, I found the person I could no longer be mad at because we were members of a family.

"But I was honestly upset when you died." He turned and looked back out at the horizon. "I didn't want to think that I was never going to get to say I'm sorry."

"Man," I said. "It's in the past, I'm sorry too."

He looked back at me. "You realize that a girl…" he trailed off.

"Yeah," I said. "It happens to the best of us."

"I haven't even talked to her since," he admitted.

"I was sure that you were talking to her that day Chris and I came to Rich's," I said. "When you said, 'you too,' at the end real quietly."

He smiled. "That was Dad."

"How's he doing?"

"He's…alive." Johnson's eyes glazed over as he stared off into the trees. He always hated talking about his father.

I picked up my notebook and tossed it to him. He snapped back into the moment and looked at it.

"The first one," I said.

He opened the book and started to read aloud.

My wrists bleed,

I see shadows in the dark.

Smoke is rising to the roof.

I begin to hemorrhage

In my feet.

The daylight all but fades away

I close my eyes

And toss and turn

But can't sleep on blood stained sheets

I followed my heart

But got lost when it stopped beating

A sharp pain shoots through my side

And I awaken to a dream

I have a cross to bear

To unload on someone who cares

Sometimes I sit and think

Searching for something to say

To the person that's never around

I want to be free

To let the scars on my back heal

I want to hear the songs of my angel

Whispered in my ear

Release the chords of life
And float into the sky
To see the unfettered world
Evolving with everyone on it
I accept change
Keep the coins for those who need it
I want to live
To die without the scar
Stigmata, stigmata
Won't you leave me alone?
Three minutes is never as long as it seems
I love you, I love you
See me as I am
Soaked through with pain
Crimson with lust
Cringing at the sound of my screams
I only move slowly
Everything else hurts.

His eyes widened as he finished reading it. "Wow," he said.

"That was what it was like to die," I said.

"Neal, I know you don't want..." he started to say, but I held up a finger to stop him.

"It was the last time I had done heroine," I said. "Anything, really."

I shook my head as I remembered the night.

"But I had been doing so much coke that I couldn't really tell if it was working or not so I kept shooting more," I said shaking my head. "That should tell you how fucked up I was."

Johnson nodded as he pulled out a cigarette and lit it. I followed suit before I continued telling him about that night.

"Suddenly, I felt like I was bleeding from everywhere, and I passed out, falling through a glass table and cutting the shit out of my back," I said, running my cigarette-free hand over an area where scars still resided. "As near as I can figure, the guys that I was with that night dropped me off at a convenience store because they didn't want to get in trouble for dropping me at the hospital. They called Chris from their cell phone and told him I was there. He picked me up and drove me to the hospital. The doctors told me that they worked on me forever. I was screaming at the top of my lungs, even though I was passed out, and at one point I flat lined. When Chris saw that I flat lined he left, he couldn't deal with seeing me die."

I paused. My arms had started to sting at the joints, and suddenly I wanted to scream. I could hear the sound of the heart monitor beeping in my ears, and I had to close my eyes tight. Tears started to build up in my eyes. I paused as I blinked them back.

"Neal, you really don't have..." Johnson started.

"I flat lined, Johnson," I said, determined to tell the story. "I was legally dead, only for three minutes, but it seemed like a fucking eternity. I remember it all. The tunnel, white light, choir of angels, life flashing through my mind, everything you've ever heard of—none of it happened. It was white and dull and fucking boring, and it took ten years away from my life."

A lump in my throat was starting to grow, making it difficult to talk. The ringing in my ears grew louder, almost to a deafening level. I pressed the bridge of my nose and closed my eyes tight, hoping that it would soon subside.

"When I came to a day later, they told me I would have to enter a drug rehab center." I looked up at the sky and sniffed the mucus that was running from my nose. "Everyone thought that I was dead because Chris had told a few people, who told a few people, and so on. I didn't want anyone to know differently. I didn't want to be alive anymore. I couldn't understand how I had done this to my life. Everything that I wanted to do or accomplish had disappeared in that moment in a sober realization that I was just another talented person who wasted it all in the pursuit of getting high."

I bit my bottom lip, looked down toward the ground, and shook my head as I closed my eyes.

"I realized that I was an unknown loser, and that I would always be exactly that. I told my parents I was okay, and that when I got out I was going back out on the road. Then they told Chris who was exceptionally relieved. He then told Rich, who told you, and so on and so on until most people heard that I was, in fact, alive."

Suddenly, the ringing in my ears subsided, and the pressure in my head quit. I wiped my eyes and took a deep breath. Then I felt the air fill my lungs for the first time in years. It was refreshing to feel alive again.

"I would give up everything for that to have never happened," I said. "I hate it when I fucking remember."

Johnson stared silently into space. I could tell that he didn't know what to say, and honestly, neither did I.

With a cautious voice, he quietly and soothingly said, "Ahhh, love."

"Ahhh, love," I repeated with a smile. But the mention of it reminded me of Chris, and the reason we weren't at Rich's. "How long will Chris be mad at me?"

"He's probably over it," Johnson said, putting out his cigarette and flicking it into the tall grass only a few feet away. He leaned back, resting on his two hands. "He was pissed yesterday, but he understands."

"Cool," I said. "Is he coming out tonight?"

"No, he said he had something he's working on that he needs to finish. He said you would understand."

I nodded.

Johnson looked at me. "And you and me?"

"We're still brothers, man. Always and forever."

He nodded as we placed the palms of our hands flat against each other's.

"2:30 a.m.," we said.

We got up and grabbed our stuff. I hadn't felt this good in a very long time. I even forgot the pain in my sides. We went to the car and got in. Johnson handed me his notebook, which he had opened to 'The Last Hit.'

"Read this for me," he said. "I want your opinion."

He started the car, and I started to read.

Last Hit

The tears build up in his eyes as he climbs to the top of the tower. He walks to the edge and scans the area. As little as he wanted to do this job, he knows that he must go through with it. He kneels down and opens his case.

He slowly lifts the black lid and stares down at the contents of the box. He carefully and slowly pulls the butt of his rifle out of the Styrofoam encasement that surrounds it, and he begins to think.

All of the people he had been hired to hit before were dirty, low people. Drug dealers, murderers, con artists, they were all on his résumé. All people that hadn't ever done anything good in their entire life. People with no emotion, people that cared only about their own personal finances and not about anyone else's well being. Hell, they didn't even care about their own happiness. All they ever wanted was to see others hurt for their gain.

This time though, this time it was different. This person cared about others, he always looked out for others. He constantly tried to make others happy even if it meant sacrificing his own happiness.

The hit man knew all this from experience. There were times when the target had given up everything so that the hit man himself could be happy.

One mistake had changed all that though. One selfish act had led to the hiring of the hit man. The reason remains unknown, but the mission stays the same.

He locks the scope into place and prepares himself in the prone position. He peers through the scope at the entryway of his target's building. The sights are set, the attitude adjusted. The only thing left is for his object to get off work and head home to see his loving family.

The tears begin to flow as his target opens the doors to his office. He watches his victim-to-be walk toward his reliable car that he has had for years, following him with the cross hairs the whole way.

As the caring man opens the door, the assassin closes his eyes and squeezes the trigger.

The bullet slices through the air as it travels toward the victim's head making contact with a violent result. Blood shoots across the front seat of the car where his children used to sit. The passenger side window shatters as the bullet passes through it. The man's body lies limp on the pavement, lifeless and empty.

The hit man stands up and wipes the tears from his eyes, inspecting the situation to be certain his job was done. He kneels down and looks at his weapon.

He slowly begins to turn the gun on himself. "Sorry, Dad."

Diary Entry XI:

Dear Jack,

    I may have been hasty in telling you Neal's dead. I talked to him today. He's okay. I couldn't imagine him going out in any way that was less amazing than Cassady's. Anyway, I gotta go, Neal's alive, I have to celebrate.

    Rich Stevens

XIV.

That night Rich and I went to the bar. Again, it was packed wall to wall with gorgeous women, and I hoped that we could find someone for Rich tonight. I had called Meagan and asked her to come and hang out with us.

The mediocre band was blasting old songs of the 1960s and 70s–regular party favorites that every band knew how to play. The crowd was eating it up. Everybody was singing along with Brown Eyed Girl, Sweet Caroline, and others of the sort.

We made our way to the bar and ordered a couple of beers.

"How are you feeling, Kid?" I asked, sipping from my beer, eyeing Rich in search of any signs of vulnerability.

"Shaky, but good," he said, as his eyes scanned the people in the bar. "How about you?"

I took a sip from my beer and looked at the ground. "Never better."

All night I had been thinking about the conversation that Johnson and I had earlier that day. I felt liberated from the harness that I had strapped onto myself years ago, and for the first time, I wasn't even having the slightest want or desire to do any drugs. I knew that I had finally rid myself of that cloak of self-destruction.

"You sure?" he asked. "You don't look it."

I looked at him and smiled.

"No, really," I said. "One day, I know you will understand how I feel right now."

"I'm sure I will," he said as he lifted his beer to his lips.

I turned back around to face the bar and looked around. Sitting at the corner of the bar, just out of Rich's sight was Jay Hooks. Jay had been Rich's dealer, and at one point, years ago, he had been mine.

Jay was the quintessential dealer. He couldn't have been any taller than five foot ten, and skinny, but you could tell by looking at him that if he wanted to hurt you, he could. His head was shaved all the way down, the only visible hair that he had was his dark, full goatee. His appearance always reminded me of an offensively stereotypical cartoon of the devil, minus the long tail, horns and pitchfork. It didn't matter how hot it got in the bar, he never removed his gray bomber jacket. He had piercing gray eyes that shot out from behind small, circular, wire frame glasses. He was constantly chewing on the filter of a burning cigarette, a nervous habit from being so jacked up all the time.

I quickly turned away before he saw me, grabbed Rich by the shoulder and pulled him away from the bar, to the hallway.

"Dude, what the fuck?" he asked, shocked from the sudden jolt of me pulling on him.

"How strong are you feeling?"

"Well, I couldn't lift a bus or anything," he said, with a tone of confused sarcasm.

"No," I shouted. This wasn't the time for jokes. I needed to know. If he couldn't handle seeing Jay, we had to leave immediately. I put my hand on his shoulder and looked him squarely in the eye. "How strong are you feeling?"

His eyes went vacant, and I knew that he wouldn't be able to handle Jay if they talked.

"Why?" he asked. His breathing had already begun to grow short and quick as he started to think about shooting up again. A small glean of sweat had appeared on his forehead.

"Jay's here," I said.

Rich turned around and put his head up against the wall. His eyes were closed, and his grip on the beer looked like it was going to shatter the glass.

"We can go," I said.

"Alright," he said, turning back around, facing me. His eyes grew wide in fear as he peered over my shoulder.

I turned my head to see Jay coming our way.

"Oh, fuck," I said under my breath.

"Rich, how've you been?" Jay asked. "I haven't heard from you in like a week."

Rich stared down at his beer. He had begun to sweat more, and the hand that was holding his beer had begun to shake.

"Yeah," he said softly. "I know."

"So what's up?" Jay asked. He had begun to eye me nervously. He didn't want to bring anything up in front of me. He assumed that I was not a big fan of his, he assumed correctly.

"Nothing, man, what about you?" Rich asked.

"Nothing," Jay said. "I was just wondering if you wanted to hang after we ditch this place."

"Umm," Rich's voice had a deep quiver to it. He looked up at me, and in his sunken dark eyes, I could see honest fear.

"No, he doesn't, man" I said.

Jay looked at me.

"Why don't you let the man speak for himself?"

I looked Jay over.

"Because *I* am here for *him*, you want to speak to him, you have to speak to me," I said. "I'm his seraphim."

"His what?" Jay asked. His eyes never waned from mine. He shook his head and waved his hand flightily in the air, pushing my comment to the side as though he didn't care. "Never mind. Rich, is this guy for real?"

Before Rich could answer, I said, "Yes."

Jay smiled and took a step back. Over his shoulder I saw Meagan walk in. She made eye contact with me and started walking over to us. I shook my head slightly to stop her. I didn't know what was about to happen, but I was going to keep Jay away from Rich with everything I had in me. She stood there watching us with nervous tension, unsure of what she should do or where she should go.

"Don't think I've forgotten you, Neal," Jay said, the smile on his face growing wide, bearing his yellowed pointed teeth. "You want to hang out tonight?"

"No," I said coldly.

"Why not? You ended up fine the last time we hung out."

A slight sting hit me in the back of the neck. I could feel rage begin to take over my body. Jay had been the one who shot me up with the last bit of heroin before I overdosed. My hands had been too shaky to put the needle in so he pushed the plunger, sending the large dose of the toxin into my veins, eventually getting to my heart and essentially killing me.

I used to have a serious anger problem. Over the years I had learned to control it, and many people had accused me of being passive aggressive as a result, but being around Jay at that moment was bringing it all back.

"Jay, I think you should leave..." I said, taking a step forward. "Now."

"Oh, come on," he said, arms raised out to the sides. "We can all go back to Rich's and do what we all really want to do."

"We're done here, Jay," I said turning around to walk away, not wanting my anger to escalate.

"Come on," he said again. "I promise, this time I'll drop you off at the hospital and not call Chris to come pick you up."

The next few minutes were a blur, all I really recall was the color red. All I know is what other people have told me. Apparently, I turned around and smashed my beer glass into his unsuspecting head in one swift movement. The shot split his head and my hand open. Blood started to pour down his face. The impact of the shot sent him crashing to the ground, blood spilling all over the floor. After that I jumped on top of him and started punching him in the face repeatedly, blood spraying from his head and my hand. All the while I was yelling curse words in what Meagan said sounded like "speaking in tongues." I had broken his glasses, his nose, and a few teeth, I figured, anyway, by the multiple cuts I had on my hand.

When I came back to, Meagan, Rich, and a few other people were holding me back, and Jay was sitting on the floor insisting to the bar manager that the police were not brought in.

The manager, a bald, self-absorbed prick, asked us to leave and told us that the tab was covered. I pulled out twenty dollars and insisted he gave it to the bartender as an apology for messing up his night. It wasn't much, but we owed him something.

We walked outside. My head was still swimming. I looked up at Meagan and smiled.

"Hi," I said.

"Hi," she said back.

"How are you doing?"

"Good," she said, kissing me on the forehead. "You really know how to show a girl a good time."

"Never a dull moment," I said.

Rich walked over and sat down next to me.

"Thanks, Neal," he said, putting his fist out, and I lightly hit it with mine.

"Anytime, Kid," I said. "Meagan, Rich. Rich, Meagan."

I leaned back as Meagan and Rich shook hands, exchanging formalities.

"So, what now?" Meagan asked.

"I don't know," I said, shaking my head.

"I don't know," Rich said, pulling a cigarette out. He put the cigarette in his mouth and lit it.

From a few feet away a voice called out, "Rich, when did you start smoking?"

We all looked up to see who it was. I didn't know the girl, but I wished that I did, which meant that she had to be...

"Claire," Rich said standing up, flicking his cigarette into the street.

Diary Entry XII:

Dear Jack,

Claire and Dylan are in love. She rarely has time to talk to me anymore. Oh well.

The great thing about people is, you can forget about them, in time.

Neal has disappeared. I tried calling him not too long ago, and he was gone. He has yet to return my calls. Fuck it.

You know my parents left me, and my grandmother. Why shouldn't my friends? Life is always kicking me in the ass. My birthday is in two days, and I have no one around to remember it. Johnson's in Jersey with Kate. Chris's... I don't even know where Chris is, I don't even know who Chris is.

I wish my parents could be here. I'd love to make them proud. Unfortunately, I never will be able to.

Anyway, Happy Birthday to me. Until next time,

Rich Stevens

XV.

The four of us walked into Rich's apartment. Rich was a nervous ball of energy. Having Claire with us made his face light up with excitement. He was talking a mile a minute about nonsensical things, and I watched in amusement as he bounced around with nervous jitters.

Meagan and I sat down on the couch, and I leaned up against her with her arm around me while Rich and Claire went back into the bedroom.

"So, that's the girl?" Meagan asked.

"That's the girl," I said. I had an odd feeling, like something was amiss or out of place in the living room. My eyes darted around searching for whatever it was.

"She's pretty," Meagan said.

"Yeah," I said. Then I realized what it was. I sat up quickly. I felt a powerful new energy inside. I suddenly had my own nervous excitement brewing in my stomach. "Chris's been here."

"What are you? A basset hound?" Meagan asked.

"No, he left something for me." I stood up and started to look around the living room chaotically.

Meagan's expression looked like she was trying to figure out if I was being serious, if I was kidding, or if I was going crazy.

"What?" she asked.

"Chris and I have a connection," I said. "I can't explain it, but we can...feel when the other person has done something...yeah, don't ask. I don't even understand it."

Which was true. Chris and I had a connection that flowed between us. Even though we had only known each other for a few years, the bond that had formed between us was extremely strong. At times it was almost as though we occupied the same space, even when we weren't in the same state. I equated it to a similar kind of bond that twins shared.

"Okay," she said, her voice letting on that she was a little freaked out by my bizarre behavior. She looked to her left at the end table. "Oh."

"What?"

"What Neal's Eyes Said To Me," she said picking up a piece of paper that was lying next to her.

"What?" I asked again, sitting back down with her.

"That's the title," she said. I reached for the paper, but she pulled it back quickly. "Nope."

"Come on, give it to me," I said, reaching for it again.

"No." She held the paper out of my reach.

"Why not?"

"'Cause I want to read it." She brought her arm back in and started to read the paper. "Do you not realize what you are doing to yourself? You're sliding down a pathway that you swore you would never venture down again. But like a dog being called to his master you came running back, tongue hanging out, eyes wide, tail wagging back and forth, not caring where the master might take you next.

"You sink deeper and deeper into a black pitted pool of hatred and self contempt. You start lying to your friends, and worse off, yourself. Believing the stories and excuses that you create, your head swims in an endless fog of confusion and bitterness, your arms flail wildly searching for support of any kind, but the longer it goes on the less support you find, and soon you're collapsed on the floor, lying in a puddle of your own piss, shit, and vomit, wondering where it all went wrong.

"From this point you look back and start pointing the finger of blame, but you know its aim is off by 180 degrees and you lie more frequently to yourself, trying to convince yourself that it was his, her, mom's, dad's fault, but never stop realizing that it is no one's fault but your own. Your friends have grown sick of all the bullshit and left you behind a long time ago chalking it up to Darwinism at its finest. You become bitter and outraged that no one you once loved is standing there for you to lean on anymore, and you try and see if you can reach the bottom of the pool.

"You dive deeper and deeper and finally hit bottom. You reach out and grab at the only weed you can find. It sinks its sharp thorns into your hand and arm, holding you down. The more you struggle to escape its grasp, the tighter it holds on, and soon you find yourself fighting for air, gasping for a chance to be forgiven for everything you promised you had quit. But no one can hear your cries of help, and you know that soon you will be inhaling that breath, which will only suffocate and end this pathetic road you've been traveling called life.

"But as the light begins to fade, and the darkness envelops every bit of your soul, out of nowhere comes a hand from a friend you thought had long since forgotten you. He pulls you from the pool and revives you. Slowly you begin to heal and feel safe enough to go swimming. Not heeding his warnings, you dip your toes in once, just to test the water, and though your friend begs you not to, soon you dive back in head first, and you're swimming for the bottom searching for the same weed you found the last time. You fear that you'll no longer have that friend to pull you out this time, and as once again the darkness envelops you, he is there to pull you out. Again, and again, and again. And I always will be, and it _pisses_ me off."

Meagan put the paper down and lightly stroked my chest. I sat there silently chewing on the inside of my lip. I was torn between two sides. I was glad that he was writing again, but I was upset that I had made him feel like a dick. I knew that this was his way of saying that he was sorry for what had happened. In all of the things he said, and all of the words he left out, he was apologizing for a life wasted. He was looking for redemption, and with that redemption, he was hoping for forgiveness from the only people that would be there for him in his time of need. He had a life's worth of people that cared about him, but not many that would sit by his side during the struggles and turmoil of addiction.

I hoped that we could talk again soon.

"I didn't know your eyes could say so much," Meagan said, ending the silence.

"Yeah, sometimes they never shut up." I smiled.

Rich walked into the living room.

"Hey, dude," he said. "Chris left a message for you. He said that Orange Moon would be ready on Monday or something like that."

"Okay," I said. I was still staring at the ground thinking about Chris's latest rant.

"What's wrong with you?" Rich asked.

I picked up the paper and handed it to him. His eyes scanned over the words, nodding at points, shaking his head at others. It was obvious that he understood everything Chris was describing. Of course, I knew everything that he was describing also.

Chris had written something that every former and recovering drug addict could associate with, written from the point of view of the person hurt the most. I knew what it was like to look Johnson in the eyes whenever I used, and he asked me not to. Rich knew what it was like when he looked Claire in the eyes. And Chris knew what it was like when he looked me in the eyes.

Rich put the paper down and rubbed his eyes.

"I think he nailed it," he said.

"Yeah, I think he did," I agreed.

Meagan looked at both of us and slightly tightened her grip around me, comforting me while I recalled the look that I had received from so many people so many times.

"You guys going to be okay?" she asked.

"Yeah," Rich said, his voice a little distant.

"How are things going in there, Rich?" I motioned to the back room.

"Good. We're having a great talk," he said, still staring at the paper. "I'm telling her everything that's been going on. She's being unbelievably understanding."

"Cool," I said. "Do you want us to, you know, leave?"

"No," he said. "It isn't like that, it's more like therapy."

I nodded.

"I got to get back in there," he said. "I just wanted to give you that message."

"Thanks," I said.

Rich turned around to walk back to his room, stopped, turned back, picked up Chris's latest rant, and then went to his room, closing the door behind him.

"It's amazing how you guys get so moved by each others writing," Meagan said.

"It's how we talk to each other. We write down what we are feeling and let the other person read it. They read it in their own voice, and it helps them understand where we're coming from. It's just easier than yelling, or crying, or pouting, or whatever. I know what Chris's saying in that. I, in a sense, connect with that emotion, and I understand better."

"Will you write me something?"

"No," I said.

"Why not?"

"I want to be able to talk to you," I said. "Like a real person."

Johnson

Johnson was born in a small town outside of Providence, Rhode Island. His father, Johnson McNamara, Sr. was a member of the Johnny Walker club, and his mother Della, was a night nurse at the local hospital. Theirs was a marriage built on their son and not on much else, if anything at all.

When Johnson was eight, Della had a mysterious accident that cost her her life. Everyone in the town blamed Johnson, Sr. even though he was acquitted of all charges. His classmates constantly reminded Johnson that his father was a murderer. Every time they went out in public, people would stop and point at them with whispers of how sad it was that Johnson was still in his father's care, just loud enough for them to hear. A year's worth of hazing and hassling led to Johnson Sr. taking Johnson away from the hostile environment and moving them to the Northern Virginia area where no one knew about the scandal.

Johnson led a decently normal childhood after moving, and up until he was thirteen he believed every word of his father's story. But as he grew, so did his

DEAR JACK: DIARY OF AN ADDICT 185

distrust and doubt, and by the age of fourteen he had become entrenched in hatred.

He started acting out and doing poorly in school. By the time he graduated he had achieved a record number of suspension days without getting expelled. When his principal announced his name, he threw on the superlative, "the most likely to eek by." Johnson gave him the finger and told him to fuck off, grabbed his diploma, took off his cap and gown and dropped them on the stage. He then walked off stage, down the stairs, and away from the ceremony never looking back, giving him legendary status at his high school, even though most people there didn't know his name. He knew that no one had shown up to see him graduate anyway.

The day after graduation, he was arrested for possession of marijuana and never touched that, or any other drug, again.

I met Johnson a few years later at the diner after one of his father's epic collisions with a Long Island iced tea truck. From my booth, I watched him chain-smoke an entire pack of cigarettes. I decided to talk to him so I walked over and joined him where he was sitting.

He was clearly upset, and although we had only just met, he didn't hesitate to fill me in on the entire story. He had come home from work, dealing cards at an underground poker game, to find his father passed out on the kitchen floor in front of the refrigerator. He carried him up to his room, careful to lay him on his side so he wouldn't swallow his puke in case he threw up. Then he went to the diner to get out of the house. As he told me, he choked back tears more than once.

Rich and Chris showed up a few minutes after he finished, and they sat down with us.

"Guys, this is Johnson," I introduced them.

They all shook hands, and our foursome was complete. Our story was finally ready to be written.

XVI.

That night Meagan and I fell asleep on Rich's couch together. It felt as though our bodies fit perfectly together as she slept against me. Her head lay softly on my chest, and her arm gripped onto my waist. My arm was wrapped around her shoulder, holding her tightly. Our legs curled around each other's, and at times, after she fell asleep, she would lightly rub her feet against mine. Her free arm was in between our bodies, and my free hand was holding hers. It was the most comfortable I had ever been while sleeping.

All night long I could smell the sweet scent of her hair, and the aroma had a therapeutic effect. Instead of dreaming about darkness and loneliness, I dreamed of happiness for the first time since I was a kid.

Some people have a fragrance that attracts others to them, different pheromones for different people. She had the scent that attracted me, and every time I breathed in that night, I felt myself smile.

Dreams are meant to be private—personal stories to be kept secret for the dreamer's own enjoyment. Also, nobody cares what someone else dreamed about. Dreams are pointless stories, small windows into the subconscious that help us see who we really are, what we really desire. In spite of all of this, I will share one moment of my dream from that night.

The sky was a magnificent blue, a few light clouds scattered throughout floating gently by. The grass was a brilliant green, and the cool breeze that passed through the field gave it a rolling effect. From across the large green tundra that stretched out in front of me, a figure slowly walked my way. After a moment or two, (who can tell, it was a dream) I made out that it was Lance. He came right up to me and shook my hand.

"Hey, Lance."

"Hey, Neal."

"How are you?" I asked.

Lance smiled and looked out to the horizon. I turned, and I could see Meagan slowly walking towards us. A smile crossed my face as she got closer.

Lance patted me on the shoulder, and I smiled bigger.

"I told you so," he said, and then he was gone.

I snapped awake and looked down at Meagan who was still cuddled into my chest. I squeezed her tighter for a second, and she let out a little sleeping moan. I smiled again as I smelled her hair and kissed her on the forehead.

"Yeah, you did, Lance," I said softly, looking down at Meagan's angelic sleeping face. "You may have been right too."

I kissed her one more time before falling back asleep.

Diary Entry XIII:

Dear Jack,

Chris is such an asshole. Who the fuck is he to judge me? How can he go from being one of my best friends, to being such a judgmental prick? Call me a junkie! He was just like me six months ago. Fuck him. Who needs that crap? He's such a hypocrite. He can suck my junkie dick. I am so done with him.

Rich Stevens

XVII.

Meagan was already awake when I woke up. She was sitting Indian style on the floor reading my notebook. I rolled over and hugged her.

"How are you doing?" I asked, kissing her on the neck. She looked at me and started reading.

Every time I close my eyes,
I fear, (or is it hope?),
that I won't open them again.
Life can't get much better than this.
The tears flow nightly,
but no one will ever see them
because I can't show emotion anymore.
I look in the mirror and wonder who I am.
I dream of a girl
who thinks I'm someone else.
To show the real me is a sin,
an unforgivable faux pas
in an unrelenting society of hypocrites
and hate mongers.
Keeping myself disguised
as someone that's together,
I move stealthily from bar to bar,

able to adapt to any social situation
yet always searching.
Searching for a soul.
Searching for a reason.
Searching for a home.
Why can't I find...anything?
A shooting star
who's about to burn away,
I fly through the night in an excellent array
of lights and explosions.
Trying to leave my mark on the hearts
and the minds of anyone who sees me.
But then again, who cares?
Who cares if I'm remembered?
Who cares if I'm noticed?
Who cares if I exist?
Who cares about me at all?"

She looked back up at me and I smiled.

"Yeah?" I asked.

She turned around and grabbed my hands. Her eyes were filled with concern as she shook her head lightly.

"Is this the real you?" she asked.

"Yeah," I said.

"Do you really cry at night?"

"Not in the actual sense of the word."

She sat on the couch next to me and lightly ran her fingers across the crease on my cheek.

"Are you still searching?"

"Yeah," I said.

"Why?"

I sat up and gently stroked her hair.

"My first 12 years of life, I lived in a van," I said. "Then my parents brought me here, and I didn't start making real friends for years. Then came Rich and then the others. Since we met, I've only been here, maybe half of the time, and they're the only reason I ever come back. If I didn't know them, I don't know if I ever would come back."

"What about your parents?"

I laughed. My relationship with my parents is a complicated one at best.

"I don't even know where they are. I bumped into them in San Francisco a month and a half ago, and even that wasn't planned. We were just in the same coffee shop...fate, I guess," I said. "They were getting ready to road trip it to New England for some chowderfest or something. They said they would call me when they got there. I haven't talked to them since."

"How do you know they're okay?"

"They always are," I said.

She leaned up against me and wrapped her arms around me tightly.

"It's so sad," she said.

"What is?"

"You've never had a place to go where you felt comfortable or welcome? A place to call yours?"

I thought about it for a second. "The road," I said, realizing the truth in that statement while also realizing how lonely it would sound to someone who had never been on it. "I've always been comfortable on the road."

"No," she said, looking for a way to describe what she meant. "When you come here, do you feel comfortable?"

"Last night I did." I didn't know why I said it, but the words came out too quickly, and I couldn't stop them.

She nodded. "Okay...before last night, was there ever a time or place when you felt like that?"

I had to think about it. I found it hard to believe that in my life I had only experienced one night in which I felt comfortable where I was staying.

"I honestly can't say," I said, lying through my teeth. Probably not the best way to start a relationship, but never had I been so nervous and full of doubt in my life.

"Wouldn't that mean that this is your home?" she insisted.

It was hard for me to comprehend that in all my years of living, the closest thing I ever had to a home was my friend's couch in his living room. Before that, the closest thing was the back of a VW bus that took me around the country. In my entire life, I had never felt comfortable anywhere I'd been. I started to wonder if it was possible to truly live without ever having a home.

"Neal, seriously, wouldn't that make this your home?" she asked again.

"I don't know," I said pulling back and away from her.

She stood up and tried to take hold of my hands, but I quickly pulled them away. I could see in her eyes that it hurt her when I did that.

"Is it at least worth a shot to see if it's a home for you?"

"I don't know," I said again, standing and taking a step back. A pit had grown in my stomach causing a discomfort that I had never felt before. My breathing had even become labored.

"What are you doing?" she asked, stepping towards me. I took another step back, away from her.

I had no idea what I was doing. My heart was pounding, I was sweating slightly, and I was having trouble concentrating. I had never felt so out of place and awkward in my life. I always relied on my words, and right now, I couldn't find any that were right. I couldn't find any at all. There was nothing I could say that would make this make sense to her, not to mention to me.

"Why are you afraid of me right now?" she asked.

"I'm not afraid of anything," I snapped. My head was spinning with questions that seemed to have no answers. I couldn't understand what I was feeling or why I was feeling that way.

"Will you please just talk to me?" she begged.

I looked around the room for an escape. I didn't know how to handle this conversation. I wanted Rich to come out of his room and interrupt us so we didn't have to continue. I knew that realistically he wasn't going to drag himself out of bed for at least another hour. Frantically, I searched for another way out of this conversation. The only thing I could see was the door so I headed straight for it.

"I have to go," I said.

"Neal, wait. Don't leave," she said, her voice full of care, pleading for me to continue the first conversation I didn't know how to have.

"I'll be right back," I said as I stepped out and the door swung shut behind me. I walked away, and I tried to breathe.

XVIII.

"I'll be right back."

I had said those words once before. They were to a girl in Seattle. We had hung out a couple of times and had gotten fucked up together most of them.

Her name was Allyson, and she insisted that she had fallen in love with me after knowing me two days. I knew then, as I know now, that no one could fall in love with me after two days, if at all. We were at this bar, drinking heavily, when I realized that she was going to ask me to stay in Seattle with her. I politely excused myself to go to the bathroom and told her I'd be right back. But I didn't go to the bathroom. Instead I walked out of the bar, got into my car, and drove down to San Francisco. Those exact words had been my escape the only time that I had ever been afraid of what might happen next.

I sometimes imagine Allyson sitting at the bar, waiting for me to come back from the bathroom. Denying the fact that I would have left her there after she had told me such a personal and honest admission. She would tell herself that no one could be so callous, so impervious, even though I would be willing to bet that she didn't know either of those words. Then slowly the realization would dawn on her. She would get up from the bar, calmly walk outside, and drive herself home, where she would break down, curse my name, and swear that she would never fall for someone again. She would hate me forever, and I don't blame her. I hate myself a little for what I did to her—it was not something I have ever been proud of, and I've felt bad about it ever since. If I could ever apologize to her, I would.

When the door swung shut behind me, I had every intention of running to my car and driving towards the sun. Instead, I found myself sitting on the steps of the apartment building and staring out toward the horizon where the highway could barely be seen. I squinted my eyes and tried to imagine driving down that highway, windows down, music blasting, sunglasses on, cigarette resting between my lips, heading for anywhere that wasn't here, but as hard as I tried, I couldn't. I couldn't do that to Meagan.

I didn't know what I was so terrified of, or why everything she asked me bothered me so much. A part of me wanted to run far away, but another part, the stronger part, kept me sitting on the steps.

It was the first time since I was in high school that I craved the advice of my parents. I wasn't sure what they would tell me. Every time I asked them for advice before, they assured me that the road held all the answers and it would guide me. How can the road hold the answer to whether or not I should be on it though? I don't know what they would say to this problem. Of course, I knew they weren't going to call me at this precise moment, no matter how much I wanted it to happen, so worrying about it did nothing but waste my energy.

Meagan came storming out of the apartment, with her bag over her shoulder and a scowl on her face, getting ready to leave. She saw me sitting on the steps and stopped.

"Rich told me you left," she said, standing there, obviously unsure of what to do in that precise moment.

"He was right in assuming so," I said. I pulled a cigarette and lit it. "I couldn't manage to get any farther than this though."

She sat down on the steps next to me. She lightly placed her hand on my shoulder and softly played with the little wisps of hair that had curled outward at the base of my head and the top of my neck.

"I'm sorry," she said. "I had no right to demand answers from you."

"No, I'm sorry," I said. "I should have been able to handle myself a little better. No one's ever asked me to stay before, or they haven't had time to anyway."

"Can we just forget that conversation ever took place?" she asked.

I looked at her through the corner of my eyes with a slight squint. She pulled her hand away from my shoulder.

"I don't think so." I shook my head and looked back out toward the horizon.

Her eyes looked down toward the ground, and she slowly nodded her head. When she looked back up at me, her eyes were filled with disappointment. I smiled and started to chuckle quietly.

She lightly slapped my arm.

"I fucking hate you," she said.

"Most people do," I said, and I kissed her gently on the lips. I stood up and took her by the hands. "Come on, let's go back inside."

We walked in the apartment where Rich and Claire were sitting on the couch watching television. Rich was demolishing a chocolate bar, which was strange because he hated sweets. I gave him a weird look and he glared at me.

"What?" he asked, licking the last remnants of chocolate off of his fingers.

"You hate chocolate," I said.

"I know," he said. "But I've been fucking craving it for some reason."

He stood up and walked into the kitchen to throw the wrapper away.

"Neal," he called.

I walked into the kitchen to meet him.

"What's up?"

"We need to talk." He motioned toward his bedroom.

I stuck my hand out signaling for him to lead the way, and we went into the bedroom, shutting the door behind us.

I sat down on the corner of the bed. Rich began to pace back and forth nervously.

"How was last night?" I asked, my eyes cautiously following him as he started to wear a hole in the floor beneath his repeated steps.

"Good," he said, continuing to pace. "We had a really intense talk."

"Cool. So what's up?"

He stopped pacing for a second, got ready to speak, and then started pacing again.

"You're going to wear a hole in your floor, Kid," I said.

He stopped right in front of me.

"This is going to be really hard for me to say," he said, his voice quivering with fear and doubt. "But I think that I should just come out and say it."

"Okay." I had no idea what he was about to say. It sounded like he was getting ready to break up with me.

"I'm hitting the road."

"Good for you," I said.

Rich took in a deep breath and exhaled while staring at the ground.

"Tuesday," he said, glancing up at me for only a brief moment.

I shot up from the bed and stood face to face with him. His eyes stayed down.

"What?" I said with a little too much emphasis.

"Tuesday," he said again, more forcefully.

"Are you fucking out of your mind?"

"Neal," he started to say.

"Sit down," I demanded, pointing to the bed. He reluctantly sat down, and now I was the one to pace back and forth.

DEAR JACK: DIARY OF AN ADDICT

"You left when you quit," he said.

"I left after a fucking month's worth of court ordered rehab," I said, trying to explain to him that our situations were not the same. "You can't do this, you're not ready!"

"Neal, you don't know what's best for me," he insisted.

"Fuck that!" I exclaimed. I wasn't arrogant enough to think that I did know what was best for him, but I feared what would happen if he left. "Rich, you, Chris, and Johnson are the only family I've got. I will fight to keep you safe. I don't want you to fail. I'm not going to allow you to throw away this past week of fucking self-torture on a bad withdrawal. They aren't over, and they don't get better for a while."

Rich stood up. We were face to face again. I could feel his breath on my nose, and I noticed the vein in his temple beginning to pulse.

"I'm not going to. I'm stronger than that," he said. "Thank you for the warning on the withdrawals though."

"You can't do this on your own, you need others to help you," I said. "What happens when you get offered some coke or heroin, and you don't have one of us around to help you? You saw how bad it got last night with Jay."

"I appreciate the confidence you have in me, Kid," he said, quietly. He walked over to his dresser and pulled out a stack of papers as thick as the Bible and tossed it down on the bed.

"That's a list of every NA meeting in every city in the lower 48," he said. "I'll be fine."

I picked up the list and flipped through the pages. I couldn't let Rich leave. I believed he had the ability to do it on his own, but I needed to be sure. I needed him there with me. The only way I could be okay was to be sure that he would be okay.

"What about Claire?"

"What about her?"

I threw the list back on the bed.

"You just going to leave her here?"

"That's what we talked about last night. She," he pointed to the door, "she thinks it's a good idea."

I turned around and walked to the door. I placed a hand on each side of the doorframe and looked at the ground, pausing to collect my thoughts.

"You can't go," I said quietly.

"Why not?" he asked. "Neal, I'm the reason you're back. You hate this city. Once I leave, you have no reason to stay here any more. You can go back to your life on the road. Living your dream of searching for a home. Running until you feel safe enough to stop."

I shook my head. He never understood that my dream wasn't to search for a home. It was to find a home. It's just that I had so much fun on my quest to find it. My hands squeezed the doorframe.

"You are the only family I have," I said, staring at the carpet that ran under the door.

"What about your parents?" he asked.

I spun around and stared at him. That was the most insane comment I had ever heard.

"I have seen Bill and Joanne for a total of two weeks in the past three years," I said. "They're still out there trying to find something that they may never find."

"Neal," he said, sitting back down on the bed. "I can't believe that you've never seen it. They aren't out there searching for anything. They found it a long time ago, in each other, and with you."

I leaned up against the door and slid down to the floor. I wrapped my arms around my knees and rested my head against the door, staring up at the ceiling. He was right. The reason they kept moving was because they loved each other, because they loved what they did. Knowing that I was out on the road, living a life that would inspire others made them happy.

"Look," I said. "I don't want you to go. I want you to stay. Because I care about you."

Rich stared at me in silence. He looked bitter and put off by my insistence that he stay. A look of realization suddenly swept over his face. I knew what he was about to say, and worse I knew he was going to be right.

"Oh my God," he said, a slight smile crossing his face.

I looked to the window, avoiding his eyes.

"You don't want me to leave because I'm your excuse to stay."

"What the fuck are you talking about?" I demanded, looking back at him.

"You want me to stay so you can figure out if this is it. Holy shit." His smile grew wider as he spoke. It seemed as though he came into a whole new light about me. "Neal Junior isn't running away this time."

"This has nothing to do with that," I said. "This is for you."

Rich leaned his head back and let out a loud guffaw.

"Six months ago, you were all for the on the road version of rehab," he said. "Admit it. You want to stay because of her."

"Fuck you."

"It's okay, Neal. Every once in a while you have to stop running."

"Fuck you," I said again, heading for the door.

"Neal, wait," Rich called, stopping me in my tracks. "It's good to stay if you want to explore new areas of life. If I had never loved, I would stay to find out if I knew what it was. But if you want my opinion..."

I turned my head halfway back, letting him know that I was willing to listen to what he had to say.

"You won't be happy here," he said. "You know you're only going to be happy on the road. It's a leap of faith either way, but when faced with the choice you have in front of you, which option seems like it will bring you the most happiness?"

I opened the door and walked out.

"Good luck on the road," I called back bitterly.

I walked through the living room toward the front door. Meagan and Claire were entrenched in a deep conversation and hardly paid any attention to me as I walked by.

I swung the front door open and stopped. Chris was standing there, hand extended for the doorknob. We stared at each other, and for a brief instant I wanted to just start swinging, beating him until he begged for me to stop. I could see in his eyes that he was terrified of what was about to happen. The moment seemed to last forever, both of us unsure of what would happen next. His eyes darted between my eyes and my hand, to see if I had formed a fist. I kept it gripped firmly on the doorknob and bathed in the humid thickness of tension.

Even though the thought of hitting him loomed in my mind, I knew I wouldn't be hitting him. I would be swinging on Rich for leaving, I would be swinging on myself for everything that I had done for the past three years, for my whole life. I would be fighting against every question that was raging through my mind. If I hit Chris, I would only be fighting myself.

His mouth opened as he started to say something, but I just shook my head and he stopped immediately.

"Come on," I said, pushing by him and running down the stairs. He let the door shut and ran after me.

"What's wrong?" he called, trying to slow me down while he caught up.

"Nothing," I shouted back to him.

I continued to run. Sweat started to drip from my forehead and ran down my chest and back. My shirt became soaked and clung to my body uncomfortably. My legs started to burn. I powered through the pain, trying to run until I stopped thinking. I could feel my heartbeat in my ears and my temples. My chest felt like it was about to explode from the force pounding from within. My tar-filled lungs stung and begged for me to stop.

I was pissed, hurt, and in pain. And the only person I had to talk to was Chris. This had become the ultimate reversal of roles. I needed his advice for the first time ever.

I stopped. I turned and waited while he caught up with me. A moment later he stood in front of me, gasping for breath.

"Neal, what the hell, man?" he asked between broken breaths that wheezed their way out of his lungs in painful asthmatic whines.

"I'm so tired, Chris," I said. My hands were shaking from the run, and my head started to throb. I shook violently. I collapsed on the grass underneath me and lay down staring up at the blue sky. I watched a few clouds drift slowly across the blue backdrop of the brisk winter afternoon.

"Have you been sleeping?" he asked, sitting down next to me.

"I'm tired of running," I said. "I'm tired of searching. I'm tired of being lost. I'm so fucking tired all the Goddamn time, and I don't want to do it anymore."

Chris didn't know what to say. He looked around nervously, trying to catch his breath, searching for something to say.

"Neal, I'm really sorry..." he started to say.

"Chris, are you listening to me?" I asked, cutting him off. "I don't want to run anymore."

"Okay." He was uneasy, unsure of what was coming.

"How do you know when you have a reason to stop?"

He looked down and a smile crossed his face.

"Is she what this is about?"

"I don't fucking know anymore," I shouted. I pickt up a rock from the ground and threw it as hard as I coula.

"Will you boys keep it down before I call the police?" the same blue haired old woman shouted from her apartment balcony.

"Will you please fuck off?" I shouted back. I hated that woman.

I could hear her shocked gasp from three floors below as she turned and slammed the door behind her.

Chris patted me on the shoulder.

"You want to know when it is time to stop?" he asked.

"Yes!" I shouted.

"When you start asking yourself questions like, 'how do I know when it's time to stop?'"

I shook my head hard. That wasn't good enough. I needed more of an answer.

"What if there's nothing there, and I stopped for no reason?"

"Neal," he said with a smile. I could tell that he was enjoying this. No one ever came to him for advice. They always came to me. Now I needed advice, and I needed him to give it to me. "You always said life is about risk. 'Take any risk that could end up benefiting your life' is what you have always told me. Well, I hate to say this at the risk of sounding cliché…"

I raised my hand to stop him. I didn't want to hear it come out of anyone else's mouth but mine.

"I know. Love is the greatest risk of all." I closed my eyes and saw Meagan. I had to open them just to stop seeing her. I didn't want her to affect this decision, but I knew that was impossible.

"Neal," he said, his voice suddenly somber. "If you want my opinion, my honest to God advice on this subject, I will give it to you. Or I will tell you what you want to hear."

I nodded.

"Honest to God opinion," I said.

"The only place that you've ever been happy is on the road," he said. "You've been on the road your whole life. This world that I live in, it's a world with rules and regulations that have to be followed. You're not a rules guy. You need to find a way to stop running while still being happy. You need to mesh the two. This world is not for you, you need the limitless freedom that is only found in the world you've created."

Chris reached into his back pocket and pulled out a stack of folded papers. He handed them to me.

"Here," he said. "I think that this was due by today."

I opened up the pages and read the title "Orange Moon."

"Actually, it was yesterday," I said, nodding.

He laughed.

"You going to hit me?" he asked.

"You going to let me?"

He shook his head. "No, not today."

I sat in the grass with Chris sitting next to me, patting my shoulder supportively, as I tapped the story against my knee, staring off at the trees that lined the apartment complex, thinking.

"So what are you going to do?" he asked.

Orange Moon

"You know that when you turn around, bend over and look through your legs, the moon will appear regular sized."

The moon was low in the dark sky. Large, blue, and beautiful. In the middle of the battlefield the lights from the city couldn't dim out the stars or the moonlight. The battlefield was always the place I went to clear my head, to talk about life with my friend.

He was quite possibly my best friend, not that I had all that many other people to confide in. He was always there for me whenever I needed to talk. I would just call him up, and we would head out to the battlefield and talk as long as it took for me to get over the most recent depression of my life. He had been loyal to me since we were five years old, when we first met. Eighteen years later and still here we were, side by side.

He had watched me grow up and change into a man. At an average 5'9", with my brown hair and brown eyes, I had grown into the average male of America, hell, my name was even Mike.

I turned and looked at him as he said this, at his large 6'2" frame, thick blonde hair, and deep blue eyes. He was the vision of the ideal male, at least that is what I gathered from seeing the covers of trashy romance novels in the supermarket.

"What?" I asked.

"If you turn around, bend over, and look through your legs, the moon will appear regular size. It has to do with the blood rushing to your head and the way it counteracts with the equilibrium in your ears and eyes. When the moon appears large, it's actually an optical illusion, your eyes are just playing a trick on you," he said, hands in pockets, looking completely relaxed in the brisk autumn night air.

"Where do you learn this shit?"

"I picked it up somewhere along the way."

I bent over and looked through my legs, giving my moon to the night sky. The moon was suddenly regular sized, small enough to hide behind the tip of my thumb. I stared at the moon in that position for a while before the alcohol and King Green that I had taken tonight decided it was time for me to continue in the down and over direction, tumbling out my somersault, once again looking at my friend.

"It's amazing how many illusions are in our lives, isn't it?" I commented, trying to sound profound.

"We all have images that we put into our lives to make them seem a little better."

I fell onto my back and stared up at the Milky Way that spanned across the night. I had to wonder if any of it was real or just something that I had created in my mind to make my life seem more bearable. With the loneliness I had thriving in my life, the possibility that there was something else out there would be the type of thing I would want to create in my head. I watched as the essence of my life climbed through the air, toward the heavens, and dissipated never to be seen again. I was going nowhere and my life showed it.

"What happened this time?" he asked.

He knew why I had asked him to join me here. He always did. He knew that something had triggered my most recent death of the soul. He knew I was searching for an answer to make it better, a piece of advice to get me through.

"You know, I don't even know this time. I was in my cubicle at the office, staring at my picture of me with the cardboard cutout of the President, and I was just hit with this sudden feeling of being completely alone."

"You talked to your parents a few nights ago, right?"

"Yeah, two nights ago."

"You probably just started remembering how it was back home. You haven't been the same since we moved out here. Probably just remembering what life was like, you compared it to your life now, and suddenly felt alone."

I pulled my glass bowl out of my pocket and lit the loaded bliss bringing my high up a notch. I felt it as the smoke moved down my throat and permeated my lungs. I hardly ever smoked, but on some nights, it was the only thing that kept me in this life. Being a social pariah has never been a lucrative career. I was determined to be as dramatic in my agony as I could without being caught by the law.

I held my agony aloft, and in the dark-cloud above my head style, I warned everyone who came near me of the danger of self-destruction. I was on the eternal search for the large orange moon, the great garner of hope and dignity from the night. The only moons that I ever saw were blue and cold, beautiful to the eye but ugly for the soul.

"Have you met anybody at work?" he asked.

"No, I don't seem to be able to meet people anymore, the office water cooler is not as popular as it was back at home."

"Maybe you need to go out, hit some bars, try to meet people that way. You need to make an effort to meet people."

"How do you know that I haven't been going out attempting to meet new people?" I asked, suddenly defensive, an obvious side effect of the pot.

"You have called me out here almost every night this week. When would you be going out to meet people?"

I rolled over on my stomach and stared at the horizon. The darkness seemed to go on forever. I tried to find a comeback for his last question but my search fell short. The only real way to tell where the night ended and the ground began was by the line of stars across the ground. I had learned long ago that I hated the day and loved the night. In the day everything is visible, and nothing is hidden in mystery. At night though, the question exists on what is real and what isn't. The shadows that are cast leave questions on the reality of everything and everyone.

"How do you take these long nights with me, talking about my asinine problems?" I asked.

"When was the last time you saw me during the daylight?"

I chuckled as I thought about it. Ever since we met, we only hung out at night. Even during our school years, he went to a private school, and I never saw him during the day. After high school ended, he worked night jobs and slept during the day. He was always willing to call out to talk to me though. How he kept his job was a mystery, especially since we moved here.

"Point well taken."

"Why are you afraid to meet new people?"

I glanced over at him, he was still standing relaxed and comfortable, completely unaffected by the night air. I shivered as a cool breeze passed through the impenetrable fortress of my windbreaker. I had no answer for the question. I hadn't always been that way. At one point I was very outgoing, very confident about who I was and what I was going to do. People respected me then, and I had a lot of fun being myself. Recently, however, my personality was the exact opposite of what it used to be. No longer confident and strong, I was now stand-offish and quiet.

"Fear of rejection," was the only applicable excuse that I could come up with. "I am afraid they would rather have a friend like you than a friend like me."

He looked down. A look of despair came across his face. Apparently what I said had hurt him but I didn't understand why. I looked up at the stars and stared into the infinite space above. A star shot across the night sky pulling a trail of light behind it. I closed my eyes and made a wish. I wished for freedom from illusion, freedom from solitude, and freedom from him.

"Are you sure it was real?" he asked.

"What?"

"The shooting star you just saw," he replied with a grin.

"Of course it was real, what else could it have been?"

"An illusion that you created just so you could make a wish. You had a desire to wish for what you did, and you may have just created the star in your mind so that you had a valid reason to make a wish."

"Of course it was real, I saw it with my own eyes."

"Mike, haven't you ever seen something, looked away then looked back only a second later to realize that it wasn't there at all? You saw it with your own eyes, but it wasn't real. Your mind will create things that trick you. It attempts to reconfirm things that you want to believe, sway issues that you are on the fence about, make you feel more comfortable in the life that you are living."

"What you are saying is that we can never really know what is real and what is not? That life is more or less all an illusion, all figments of what we believe, or want to believe?" I asked cynically.

"Exactly."

I jumped to my feet, and a quick rush shot through my body from rising too quickly. I shook my head, attempting to regain composure on my body. A sense of anger and fear overcame me as I pondered the possibility that most of my life had been a farce. I couldn't tell if anything was real or just a part of my mind that I had dragged out to make everything seem real. I didn't want to accept the fact that life was not as real as I had hoped.

"What is the point of living if nothing is really there? Why would we live in a life that isn't real?"

"Each of us has an ideal form of life that we are striving for, it doesn't matter that it is only in our mind. We crave it; we need it. It isn't real, but we strive to achieve it. We don't just stop living because we believe that all of our hard work will result in a better reality. It doesn't even matter that we could sit back and, with a clear head, see that none of it is real."

"I don't see my life getting better with my illusions and dreams. It keeps going further and further down the pathway of loneliness and solitude. What if I just ended it all? What would change if I left this world of falsehoods and illusions forever?"

"In all honesty, nothing would change. Your parents would feel sadness and depression for a while, but soon they would create some image of happiness that they would believe in and rely on to get them through the days. They would never forget about you, or forgive you for that matter, but they would eventually get over the untimely passing of their son and go on living their lives."

"And what about you?" I asked.

"Mike, you know what would happen to me."

I realized what he meant by that, nothing would happen to him. He would go on with his life as though nothing had ever changed. His illusions made his life better, and he could fill the void of me leaving with one of his illusions. He had done it his whole life, he was a master at creating false truths. He had always been happy even though his life was never great. He thrived on his illusions and loved them. He could get through any problem that he faced. Even the brutal and grotesque death of his parents never took him down that much. He lived through it and turned it into motivation to make him strive harder for a better life that he had given to himself. And it pissed me off.

"How do you do it?" I asked. "How do you go through life without worrying about the defeats, the pain? Why does everything roll off your back like…?"

"…water on a duck?"

"Yeah, exactly."

"I control what I conjure up, I control what I believe. You make things up spontaneously, without thinking about what your illusions will result in. I think about my illusions before I make them, I try not to create anything that could possibly hurt me or bring my hopes up to a level that I could never reach."

"And I do?"

"Yes, you create things that set the bar too high. Things that make your life seem lower than what it truly is."

"How do you know what I make up in my mind?"

"The same way you know everything I create in my mind."

That is when it hit me, like a punch from the heavyweight champion. Suddenly everything was explained. The reason I never saw him during the day, why he was always there for me, why he seemed to live such a great life. I had created him in my mind. He was an illusion that I had made as a child. Suddenly I understood why he always hung out with me, why he didn't know anyone else, or at least never talked about them. He was my imaginary friend, and for 18 years, I had treated him like a real person.

"You never can tell what is real and what isn't," he said.

"You should be able to, things shouldn't seem that real."

I was having trouble breathing. The only friend that I have had for my whole life was an illusion, someone that I made up for some reason, a way to make my life seem somewhat better.

"Why?" I asked stunned. "Why is it like this? Why do I believe it?"

"Your life is the definition of average—your build, your job, even your name. You are at the paramount of ordinary. I am not. I have the exceptional build, a job that you only wish that you had, and the looks of a Greek god, and I have a super human ability to make anything work toward my advantage. You tell me why."

He was right, of course. I made him up so that I would have someone above ordinary to talk to. Someone who was extraordinary to balance out my mediocrity. It was because of him that I couldn't make friends anymore. I was trying too hard to live up to the standard that he set. His existence was fatal toward my social recognizance. Until I could get rid of him, I would always feel as though I wasn't good enough to be around others.

"To make up for my inadequacies," I said quietly.

"If that is what you believe, then yes, that is the reason why. You and I are here for whatever reason we choose to be here. It is all about illusion. You can be whatever you would like to be in your mind. If, in your mind, you are an inadequate little peon, then that is what you will be. But if you believe in yourself and what you can accomplish, then you can be whatever you want to be."

"And what do you want to be? I want to know what you want."

"I want to be happy. I want to see that my friends are happy. I don't want people to be upset with who they are or what they do. I want people to realize that life is what you make of it."

"You want to make sure that your friends are happy? That is why you are destroying my life by telling me that nothing in it has ever been real? You want me to be happy?"

"Yes, by learning this, you learn that you can improve on your life using only your mind. Your mind is a very powerful thing and can change so much on the way that you perceive life."

The moon had fallen lower in the sky. I turned and looked as the bottom tip of it rested upon the horizon. I knew that shortly the sun would be rising in the east. The end of this night of revelations was nearing.

"You know everything that I think?"

"Yeah, just like you know everything that I think."

"What number am I thinking?"

"79," he said with a smile.

I was aghast as the two minutes and thirty-six seconds of the moon setting began. The blue was gone, and the moon now shone with a deep orange hue. The great garner of hope and dignity from the night was staring right in my face. I looked down in shame, for no longer did I deserve hope nor dignity. I realized at this moment how truly alone I was. A tear began to drip down my cheek and off my chin. I tried to wipe it clean before he saw it but to no avail.

"Mike, why are you crying?"

"Because I know that I have no real friends in this world, only the made up images of you. I created someone to trick myself into believing that I had a friend, someone that would follow me to the end of the earth. I created you. I created someone that I wished I could be. I guess to be honest, I have known all along. I just never wanted to come to grips with the fact that nobody alive wanted to be close to me. Even my parents and I were never very 'Cleaver.' It makes perfect since that I made you up as a child. I needed someone to rely on. I guess I still do, eh?"

I turned and looked at him. A smug grin was plastered across his face. He still appeared comfortable in the frigid air. I made up this person that could be bothered by nothing. He was the cool guy, the guy that I wanted to be.

"Mike, what is your address?" he asked me.

"What?"

"What is your address?"

I thought about it for a second. I couldn't remember it. I tried to shake my head clear from all the substances that I had put into it tonight, but that didn't help. I couldn't remember what the street name was. Before I could open my mouth to tell him, he asked, "Where do you work?"

"At the computer company," I answered.

"Well, what is written at the top of the checks that they give you?"

Once again I blanked. I had been with this company for a year and could not remember the name of it. I was completely flustered by all that had happened tonight. I just wanted to go back to my home, wherever it was, and go to bed. I would call out sick to work tomorrow.

"I don't know, I can't remember."

"Does this strike you as odd?"

"Yeah, a little, nothing to be worried about. Everything is in our mind, right?"

"Mike, when is your birthday?"

He wouldn't even let me try to answer this one. He knew that I didn't know, he knew that I couldn't know.

"You don't know, Mike, do you? You want to know why?"

I looked at him confused and somewhat frightened. I wasn't sure how to answer that question.

"Mike, the reason that you don't know the answers to these questions is because *I* am not the imaginary one, you are."

A sudden chill came over me. I realized that I hadn't changed my whole life. It explained why he was my only friend. And why he reminded me of things that I didn't seem to know. And why someone so extraordinary would be with someone like me. Everything I had ever done was exactly average. I graduated in the exact middle of my class; I was getting paid the average yearly income; I was always the average height, the average build. I wasn't anything special. That was why I was created.

"How do I know that is true?" I asked defensively.

"Because, Mike, I am not thinking of you anymore."

Diary Entry XIV:

Dear Jack,

    I don't think I want to do this anymore. There is no point in writing you. Goodbye my old friend.

    Rich Stevens

XIX.

I put the story down and nodded.

"I like it," I said.

"Thanks," he said as he patted me on the back reassuringly. He could tell how lost I was at the moment.

"You really are a good friend, Chris," I said, pulling out a cigarette and lighting it.

"I know," he said. "It's basically my only good quality."

"That's true," I agreed, with a smile on my face.

He punched me in the arm. "Dick."

"Technically," I said, rubbing my arm, "that would be Johnson."

He laughed and took my cigarette from me, inhaled a lungful of smoke, and handed it back as he exhaled.

"How are doing?" I asked. "I know that we have all been paying attention to and taking care of Rich, but what about you? You staying clean?"

He nodded. "Yeah, don't worry, I'm clean."

"But how are you doing?" I asked.

He shrugged and nervously bit his lower lip.

"I know why we're all here for Rich," he said. "I get it. He needs the support. And I know that I seem like all I ever need is support from people. But this - this is different. It sucks. It's hard. I have to work at it every day. I've almost broken down a few times, but I won't, not again."

I could see that he had goose bumps at the thought of using. All the hairs on his arm were standing on end, and he had developed a slight shiver as he talked.

"But," he continued, "I did this to myself. I can beat this on my own. There are moments I want to scream. There are moments I want to cry. There are moments I want to run away. But I keep waking up and going through the motions of my day, knowing that tomorrow will be a little easier than today was, and if I ever feel like I'm about to break, I have you to make sure I don't."

He swallowed hard and nodded, wiping a tear from his eye. I patted him on the back reassuringly.

"I'm proud of you," I said.

"Thanks."

"Come on," I said, motioning up toward Rich's apartment. "Let's go back up."

Chris and I walked into Rich's apartment. Meagan and Claire were still sitting on the couch, engrossed in what I could only assume was the same conversation. As we walked by, they once again barely noticed our presence.

We walked right in to Rich's room. Rich was sitting on the bed writing in his notebook. He looked up at us as we entered. Chris quickly snatched the notebook out of his hands before Rich could react.

"What's this?" Chris asked.

"Give it back," Rich said, trying to grab it from Chris who quickly took a step back.

I leaned up against the wall and watched them play their childish game. I folded my arms across my chest and shook my head.

"Give it back," Rich said again, standing up to take it. Chris turned his back to Rich and stretched his arm out, blocking Rich's reach.

"You have an angel heart," Chris started to read.

"Stop it," Rich said, lunging at the book. Chris turned away as Rich tripped and fell to floor.

"But you hide behind a pair of devil eyes," Chris went on.

"Fuck you, Chris," he said, still sitting on the floor.

"What? Are you embarrassed by it?" I asked, looking down at him.

Rich shot me an evil eye, then looked back at the floor. Chris smiled as he started over.

"You have an angel heart,
but you hide behind
a pair of devil eyes.
I'm stuck as a child,
lost in a world
where you despise me
for being obtuse.
Just because I'm me.
The swelling looks painful,
I just want your support.
My friends all faded away,
back when I could be one

but was consumed with the truth about money.
There is no good society,
and everyone talks back.
Helter skelter,
anyway you want it.
We're so self-righteous.
Welcome to the Titanic,
we're all gonna die.
What came first,
music or misery?
Nostradamus was wrong,
Cobain was right,
entertain us.
Random thoughts,
laid out on a page,
seemingly meaningless.
like most lives do.
George Bailey can tell you,
life matters.
Unless I don't want it to.
I forget people,
they'll forget me.
Don't think you're different.
I already forgot.
Who are you?
I'm sorry I'm me,
childish and such.
You kiss so well,
I'm not supposed to
think about that though.

We're in the first third,
but I feel like
it's the last one.
Don't look at me
with your devil eyes.
Temptation breaks me down
every night I'm with you.
My soul slips away.
Why am I a good guy?
When am I mean?
I wonder if I can cry anymore.
God bless you, Mr. Junior,
you are the king.
The sun is set.
To see a specter isn't everything,
never lift this veil,
my eyes can't handle the light.
I'm sorry I'm me."

I pulled a cigarette out and lit it. Chris tossed Rich the notebook and sat down on the bed. Rich closed the book and tucked it under his arm. He looked up at me. I turned my head away.

"That was uplifting," Chris said.

"Like anything any of us has ever written has been uplifting," I said, walking across the room to ash.

Chris nodded his head in agreement.

"Why is that?" Rich asked.

"Because we're all too fucking afraid to realize that life might actually be good," I said. "We walk around wearing crimson colored glasses..."

"Crimson colored?" Chris asked.

"Yeah, as in not rose colored, but the color of blood and death," I said.

"Another uplifting thought," Rich said.

I gave him the finger.

"We walk around with crimson colored glasses, finding all that's shitty with the world, seeing all the things that suck"

Rich stood up and put his notebook on the dresser.

"That's cause everything does suck," he said, grabbing a pack of cigarettes off the dresser and lighting one.

"How the fuck do we know that?" I asked. "We're still young enough to make this life whatever we want to make it, and ever since we met each other we've been saying that girls suck..."

I looked at Chris who nodded.

"Sobriety sucks, parents suck," I said, looking at Rich, "or being here sucks. We've never even tried to look around and see the good in anything."

"We're not positive people," Chris shrugged.

Rich reached his hand out and cocked his head to the side, showing his support of the statement.

"He's right, Neal," Rich said, taking a long drag off the cigarette. "There are positive people, and there are negative people. We are of the latter."

"It's not just that, even the most negative people can find one good thing in this world," I said. "We've never found anything. Chris, even when you were with Michelle, you fucking hated it, but you said you loved her."

"How wrong was I?" he asked.

Rich smiled. I could see that in his mind he was thinking about how that particular relationship changed everything. Deep down he probably knew that it was bound to happen anyway, he could pinpoint that one event as the beginning of it all.

"That *was* fucking stupid of you," he said.

Chris nodded and shrugged.

"What are you saying?" Chris asked me.

"We never find anything good in this world because we haven't found or heard what we need," I said.

Chris and Rich looked at each other, confused. I thought about what I had said, and suddenly I was confused. I knew what I was trying to say, but I couldn't find the right words.

"Okay," I said. "What does Johnson need more than anything else in this world?"

They looked at each other again and shared another look of confusion.

"It's not a hard question. What does he need?"

"To know his dad's being honest," Chris said.

"His mom," Rich said at the same time.

"Alright," I said, hoping that they understood what I was getting at. "If his father decides to be honest, or proves that he has been honest, do you think Johnson would be able to adopt a more positive view on life? Or at least find one good thing in his world?"

Suddenly I realized what I was saying and what it meant. Chris and Rich looked at me. I couldn't even figure out where this was all coming from.

"Are you saying that if I get what I really need, I won't see things in such a negative light?" Chris asked.

"Well, yeah, I guess so," I said timidly.

"Just because I find what I need doesn't mean that I'll begin running around like some fucking club kid on ecstasy saying that I love everything," Rich said.

"Not everything," I insisted. This was apparently harder than I had expected it to be. "But you may find something that you don't hate so Goddamn much."

"So...what do I need, Neal?" Chris asked.

This was going to be difficult. Rich's needs were easy to explain but harder to solve. Chris's were hard to explain, and he wouldn't want to accept it. He had to stop seeing his life the way he did. He needed to hear the truth —about himself, his life, and the decisions he had made. I knew I had to be the one to tell him.

"Chris, the truth is, you don't need anything," I said, a sigh leaving my lips. "You need to realize that only one thing has ever gone wrong in your life."

Chris looked at me, somewhat shocked that I would say that. He had always held this poetic vision of his life, that he was a tortured artist that wouldn't be appreciated until he was gone. Everything that happened to him in his life, positive or negative, became the next big thing that would make his life better or destroy it. This was exactly why he was so easily swayed into using drugs and why he will forever struggle with heartbreak and addiction.

"A girl broke up with you and it broke your heart," I said. "A long time ago. You haven't fully trusted or opened up since but will tell people that you love them so you can attempt to duplicate that same feeling. Not the feeling of love and connection, but the feeling of depression that eats away at you when your relationship inevitably ends."

Chris could do nothing but stare at me. I could tell he was getting angry about what I had just said. Eventually he would say something passive aggressive to show me his contempt, but I knew I had to keep going. He had to hear it all.

"You have a loving, caring family," I said. "A family that's there for you. You had a good job, which you could get back if you were so inclined. You've got friends."

I motioned to the people in the room.

"You aren't hurting for money. You're loaded with untapped talent," I continued. "You have a firm grasp of what is considered wit, you're funny on the very rare occasion."

His face remained carved as a statue. Even my joke didn't make him crack a smile. This was probably very difficult for him to hear.

"One girl fucked you up years ago, and you should be over it by now," I went on. "There is nothing wrong with you except you *want* to be unhappy for some unknown reason. You cling to sorrow like a coma patient clinging to life. I don't understand it, but I suppose, if you wanted to be happy instead, none of us would be here right now."

Chris's eyes went vacant. It appeared as though I had pulled his life right from him and dangled his disembodied soul before his eyes while telling him that he didn't deserve it anymore. I could see that he wanted to tell me to fuck off, but he couldn't tell me I was wrong. His mouth opened on occasion, making him appear like a fish that had been hooked, as he tried to find the words to tell me I was wrong.

A sound left his mouth, which was probably the beginning of his retort, but Rich cut in. "And what do I need?"

I turned around to look at him, relieved that he had cut Chris off. Chris, though sweet and friendly on the outside, stored a pile of venom and bile deep inside of himself. When he said things to hurt, they hurt. He would start to talk and by the time the words left his mouth, he knew he had gone too far.

"Rich, I have no idea what you need. You have no family, with the exception of those present in this room and Johnson. Everyone that you've ever been close to has…left," I said, trying my hardest to be tactful. "Because of this you have trouble getting close to people, with the exception of us." I motioned to Chris and myself, hoping it was understood that Johnson was included. "You've been an addict for years in a futile attempt to detach yourself from anything in this world that is real. I can honestly say that I don't know what you need. I believe that you have to find that out on your own…"

I paused because I did know what Rich needed. It was the same thing that I had always needed. It was the only thing I've ever really known. And it was the only thing that showed me the absolute and infinite beauty that this world can possess.

"Which is why...you should go," I paused, "on the road." The last few words broke from my mouth and I couldn't believe that I was actually speaking them.

Rich and I had too much in common for me to deny that we were basically the same person. My parents were gone. His were never coming back. We dealt with abandonment issues, and like how I never was able to truly open up to a woman, Rich was emotionally incapable of trusting anyone. We both searched for the answers in drugs. We tried to answer our questions on paper by ranting about the world and how bad it was. I couldn't deny the fact that since I needed the road to find out what I needed, he did too. I knew that he could find the answers on the road, and I knew he wanted my approval to do it.

"You're telling me to go?" he asked, stunned, his eyes suddenly alive.

"Yeah," I said morosely. I knew that I was now going to have to make a very hard decision. A decision that I didn't want to make, wasn't ready to make. Not yet anyway.

He walked over and gave me a hug. I felt him start to cry. Chris sat on the bed, still shocked by what I had said about him.

"Rich," Chris said. "Do you agree with what Neal told me?"

Rich released his grasp on me and wiped his eyes.

"Yeah," he said. I could tell that it hurt him to have to be painfully honest with Chris too. It never feels good to shatter a friend's perception of the world. "I've always wondered what was so bad in your life that made you so upset."

Chris looked at the ground. I could tell that he was going through every memory of his life, trying to find something to use as an example for why his life was a horrible fucking mess, but he knew, as did Rich and I, that apart from Becky, nothing bad had happened to him.

There was a knock at the door and Rich went to open it. Claire and Meagan walked in.

"What are you boys doing?" Claire asked, looking at Chris sitting on the bed, staring at the floor.

Rich realized that they had not been introduced and went ahead with the formalities.

"Claire, Meagan, this is Chris," he said.

Chris looked up from the ground. The stone face was gone and was replaced with vitality. His baby blue eyes lit up with a natural sparkle. He was glowing. There was a completely different aura about him, something magnetic, intriguing. I slowly saw what the difference was. For the first time since I met him, Chris had a real, genuine smile on his face.

"Hi," he said, standing up to shake their hands.

"Hi," they said back.

"So what now?" Chris asked, looking at me. All anger that was squatting in his eyes gone, replaced by acceptance and friendship. I should have told him his issues years ago. He seemed like a brand new person.

"I don't know," I said, thinking for minute. Then an idea hit me. I looked at Chris and Rich and smiled. We all nodded. "We should probably get Johnson over here."

"I'll call him," Rich said, pulling his phone out of his pocket and walking out of the room.

I turned to Meagan and Claire and smiled.

"What?" Meagan asked nervously.

"Will you all go get us a shit load of beer and stuff?" I asked, flashing a smile.

Chris cleared his throat behind me.

"And maybe two friends?" I asked.

Chris coughed.

"Who are as cool as you two are?"

Chris cleared his throat again.

"And as beautiful?"

They both gave me a look that showed they appreciated the compliment but also saw that I was being extremely sycophantic. I flashed an overly sarcastic grin and said, "Please?"

"We'll be back," Meagan said kissing me on the cheek before she and Claire walked out.

"I can't wait," I called to her. I turned to Chris and smiled.

"How did they become such good friends that quick?" Chris asked. "They just met each other like three hours ago."

"Do you remember when we met?" I asked. "We knew each other for five minutes before we went to the diner."

Chris nodded, remembering how quickly we had become connected.

"Hey, Neal," he said.

"Yeah?"

"It's going to be one memorable night."

Neal

I was born in the backseat of a VW bus on Route 50 near San Francisco. My parents were traveling writers, or as almost everyone else called them, hippies. My dad, Bill Junior, and my mom, Joanne Lenton, gave me my name, Neal Lenton Junior, and taught me about the freedom of the open road at a very young age. Until I reached the age of 12, I was never in a city for longer than a month.

I was, I guess I would call it, van-schooled until Bill and Joanne decided that we should settle down so I could find the true joys of friendship and other things that I never experienced until after high school.

Throughout most of high school, I was an outcast, pretty much until my last day there. None of the other kids understood why I was constantly writing in a notebook, or why, not coming from a military family, we moved so much, or why I called my parents Bill and Joanne, or why they weren't married. We were looked at as freaks because Northern Virginia had never seen parents show up to a P.T.A. meeting wearing "Legalize Marijuana" t-shirts. The other students' parents hated my parents so most of the students hated me. The ones who did pretend to like me were the stoners who thought maybe my parents would hook them up with the occasional free weed.

The administration hated me because of my parents, and most of the teachers were in the same boat. My English teacher hated me because I knew more about literature and writing than she did, and soon going to school was a chore that I wasn't going to do anymore. I started taking G.E.D. classes at night, continuing to go to school during the day. I took and passed the test when I was 17.

The next day I walked into school wearing a shirt that said, "Legalize All Drugs," with the picture of a syringe in the middle of it. When a teacher told me to remove it, I ripped it off, displaying the Bill of Rights drawn on my chest with a big red circle around the first one. On my back was a picture of a smoking bong surrounded by the phrase "fuck off high school," which Bill had drawn for me and which everyone saw as I ran through the hallways. That day I became a legend in my high school and was no longer an outcast. Ironically, it was that day that I embraced being an outcast.

I went straight home, packed my bags, and told Bill and Joanne I would be back. I don't think they had ever been more proud of me. I got into my car and left for six months. I didn't know where I was going or what I was doing. I only knew I wanted the road under me. So I drove, with no destination in mind and with no idea how I was going to make money or survive. It was a learning process, and slowly I figured out how to live on the road.

I grabbed life by the wheel and made the stretches of black asphalt the comforting walls of a home. Every mile I logged on my car was another problem solved. Every oil change I performed on the side of a highway was an opportunity to reflect on all I had accomplished. It didn't matter where I had gone, what mattered was that I had found the ultimate therapy in the open spaces that were available. Life was beneath the four wheels of my car, and I travelled on them trying to experience everything life had to offer.

When I got back, Bill and Joanne were gone, but the house was still there for me.

Two weeks later, I met Chris at the coffee shop.

XX.

Johnson arrived half an hour later. Claire and Meagan were still out on the hunt for two friends that met our high standards. Chris sat on the couch anxiously awaiting their return. Any time someone would walk up the stairs of the building, he'd stand up and practically run to the door.

"Calm down, Brother," I said, after one of his sprints to the door.

"Do you know how long it's been?" he asked, looking at me with a hint of desperation in his eyes. "A year."

At first I wasn't sure whether or not he was joking, but his face remained somber, and I suddenly felt for him.

"What about....?" I made a fist and pantomimed jerking off.

"Lost its appeal after six months," he said. "And I started chafing real bad. Now I only do it maybe once a week."

Johnson was walking by right at that moment, and he stopped when he heard Chris's last statement.

"Chris, you need to learn to think before you say these things."

Chris just shrugged. He wasn't worried about what Johnson or I thought about his masturbation habits. Rightfully so, but still slightly disturbing.

"Chris," I said. "Women can sense your desperation to...um..."

"Build a bridge to Terabithia," Johnson said, his face beaming at his euphemism.

I looked at him, shocked at the crassness of the joke but also proud at its wittiness.

"Right," I said, pointing to Johnson trying to figure out how I felt about his entendre. "I'd suggest taking a sabbatical in the bathroom to calm yourself down just a bit."

"Wasn't it Hemingway who thought you only had so many doses of 'baby batter' in you?" Chris asked.

"I think so," I said. "Why?"

"Well, I'd hate to waste them all at such a young age," he said.

"You're still relatively young, Chris," Johnson said. "I'm sure you'll be fine for another year or so."

I pushed Chris into the bathroom and shut the door behind him. My body shook in disgust as I involuntarily thought about what would go on in there.

"Makes you sick, doesn't it?" Johnson asked, walking toward the living room.

We sat on the couch and shared a body convulsion as the picture entered our minds again. There was a light slapping sound coming from the bathroom.

Rich came out of the bedroom and stopped in mid-stride as he heard the noise.

"What the fuck is that?" he asked, pointing at the bathroom door.

"Chris had to relieve some pressure," I said.

"That's fucking disgusting. Why would you tell me that?" he said, sitting on the couch between Johnson and me. "When are they going to be back?"

"Soon, I would assume," I said.

Rich nodded and lit a cigarette.

"This is Meagan, from the bar?" Johnson asked, and I nodded. "Wow, Neal. What's it been, four days? Is that a record for you?"

I raised my middle finger, which only made him laugh.

"And this is Claire," he continued. "As in, 'Claire'?"

Rich nodded this time, then looked at him, as if daring him to say something smartass.

"They're bringing friends, right?" he asked again.

Rich and I both nodded this time as the front door swung open, and Meagan, Claire, and their two friends walked in.

The three of us stood to greet them. Meagan came over and hugged me, then kissed me fully on the lips, possibly to mark her territory in front of the new girls.

"Neal, this is Kayla and Erica," she said.

Kayla was the shorter of the two, not much over five feet tall. She had rich, dark hair, olive skin, and full lips. She looked very Mediterranean, and I thought I caught a hint of an accent when she said, "Nice to meet you, Neal."

Erica was the "Girl Next Door." Shoulder length blond hair, blue eyes, extremely red lips—she reminded me of a farmer's daughter, the one that ended up getting someone shot at with a rifle while running off the wooden front porch in his underwear. Pants, shoes, and shirt clutched firmly to his chest as he prayed the farmer had a bad shot.

"How are you?" she asked in a mousy little voice that seemed to fit the image.

"I'm great," I said. "This is Rich, and this is Johnson."

They were exchanging formalities when the bathroom door opened and Chris walked out.

"Neal, you were right. I am much more relaxed, now that I..."

He'd just walked into the living room and saw everyone staring at him. Johnson, Rich, and I sat there with grins on our faces. Chris's face was caked in embarrassment.

"Now that I took," he paused and gave it another shot, "...tried to...um."

Then he just gave up and shook his head.

Johnson, Rich, and I shared a muffled laugh. The girls just looked confused.

"Ladies, this is Chris," said Rich, still trying not to laugh.

"Hey," said Chris, his face turning a fierce shade of red around his smile.

I got the idea that Kayla found his embarrassment to be very cute. But Chris, as always, was oblivious.

Diary Entry XV:

Dear Jack,

This is it, the final entry to you. One last story or tale before I send myself off silently into this dark life. Claire and Dylan have ended their run, I think he broke her heart, for she hasn't said more than two words to anyone since the break up, or at least to me. I dream about being with her, and at times I think I may love her, but I don't know if I'm capable of loving. I think it could be everything that I inject myself with that makes me believe a real life is possible.

I often wonder if you can even begin to know all of the confusion I live with every day. I have no family, no friends, just my dealer, who is only there for me because I give him money everyday. I don't remember the last time I even left the house. I now know what Burroughs was really describing in "Naked Lunch" and how "The Subterraneans" came out the way it did. I wish things made sense...life is just so damn confusing.

Anyway, I am off to figure it all out, or die trying. Goodbye, Jack, maybe if any of this shit begins to make sense, we can converse again. If you were breathing, I would tell you not to hold it.

Rich Stevens

XXI.

The get together was going well, and Meagan and I decided to take a moment to ourselves. We snuck out on the patio while the others were sitting around, talking and drinking. Once outside, I kissed her before she had time to say anything.

"What was that for?" she asked, when I finally let her loose.

I took a sip of my beer and stared out over the city skyline that was lit up.

"Rich is leaving," I said, pulling a cigarette out of my pocket.

She placed her hand on my shoulder and gently squeezed. There was an ominous, nervous feeling between us just then.

"When?" she asked. I could hear a stifled crack of fear in her voice.

"Tuesday," I mumbled.

"Oh."

"He's not ready. But I can't stop him." I took another sip of my beer.

"Is that really why you're upset?" she asked.

"Yeah. Why else would I be?"

"Maybe *you're* not ready," she said.

She was very astute. I had to hand it to her.

"I'm ready," I said. "But I wasn't ready when I was where he is now."

She looked at me confused. I wasn't even sure what I was saying anymore. My mind was swimming with questions.

"What are you talking about?"

"I don't know." I flicked my barely used cigarette over the railing. "What are you talking about?"

"I'm not sure," she said, giving me a look out of the corner of her eye.

I gave her the same confused look right back, then shook it off and smiled.

"Now is it just me," she started, "or does Kayla have a thing for Chris?"

I peered in at them through the window and laughed. Kayla kept finding reasons to touch Chris's shoulder or knee. She was laughing at his jokes, even though I knew that he had no sense of humor. Chris just went on talking about whatever random topic came into his mind.

"Yeah. No doubt," I said. "I don't think he realizes it though."

Meagan just shook her head. "How could he not?"

"Chris's always oblivious to things like that." I shrugged. "He doesn't pick up on it, doesn't see it."

"Should we give him a little push in the right direction?" she asked.

"Not yet," I said, pulling her close to me. I started kissing her neck and behind her ear.

"Are you trying to get me to follow you to the ends of the earth?" she asked, her voice a mixture of euphoria and excitement.

"I definitely wouldn't complain if you decided to," I said, in between kisses.

She pulled her head back and smiled up at me, then pulled me in closer and kissed me again.

"What are you doing tomorrow?" she asked when we'd parted.

"Coffee shop, I think."

"What do you guys do there all day?"

I looked at her stupidly and shrugged my shoulders. "Drink coffee."

She hit me lightly and scowled.

"God, I hate you," she said, then she took me by the hand and led me back inside.

We walked into the living room where everyone was sitting. Erica looked up at us as we walked in.

"Neal, are you a writer too?" she asked.

"Yeah," I said.

"Is that all you do?" she asked.

"Yeah," I said again.

"One day, Neal is going to write a book about all of us," Chris said, "and make us all household names."

"He flatters me," I said. "In truth, our names will only be known in some of the houses."

"You see that man there, Erica," Johnson said, nodding toward me and pointing at me with his beer bottle. "He hasn't been in any one city for longer than a month since he was 17. And it shows in everything he's

ever written. Which is why he wins contests and gets
published in magazines but has never been able to sell a
collection."

Erica looked confused, and I would have bet that it
wasn't an uncommon look for her. I looked at Meagan
nervously after Johnson said I had never been anywhere
longer than a month. I noticed a brief look of worry cross
her face.

"I don't get it," she said.

"Nobody wants to buy a book of poetry. It doesn't sell
well enough unless you are exceptionally famous," I said,
putting my arm around Meagan for reassurance. "My only
option is self-publishing, and I don't want to do that."

"Why not?" Kayla asked.

"It feels like selling out to me," I said. "I know that
there's the argument that it is the exact opposite of selling
out, but it seems like the last bastion for someone who
can't find a home for his or her work."

Johnson's phone started to ring. He gave his phone a
confused look, then walked out of the room. I motioned
for Chris to follow me into the kitchen.

"What's up?" he asked when we got there.

"You don't see it at all, do you?"

"See what?" he asked, truly clueless.

"That Kayla's trying to hook up with you."

"What?" he asked, stunned. He peered cautiously into
the living room. "Are you sure?"

"Oh, Jesus," I said, waving my arms in disbelief. I
thought Meagan might be able to tell him better. "Meagan,
will you come in here, please?"

"Yeah?" she asked, walking into the kitchen.

"You tell him," I said.

"What, about Kayla?"

"Yeah."

"Chris, she is so into you."

"How can you tell?" he asked.

Meagan just looked at me. "Is he serious?"

I nodded. I looked Chris in the eyes and placed my hand on his shoulder. "You need to grow a sack. Get out there and..."

Johnson had come walking into the kitchen. His eyes were hollow, vacant. He looked ready to collapse.

"What's up, Buddy?" I asked him.

His face was the picture of despair. A slight sheen of sweat had broken out around his forehead and eyes. His hands shook ever so slightly as he tried to find the counter to put his phone down.

"My dad's in the hospital," he said as his legs gave out. He sat on the kitchen floor and tried not to cry.

XXII.

I sat off to one side of the waiting area while Johnson argued with the nurse about seeing his father. Around the room, there were a number of patients waiting patiently to be treated.

There was a young boy around the age of six with dark circles around his eyes, leaning against his mother's breast, wheezing every time he breathed. The high-pitched squeal came from his throat with every labored breath. Sweat covered his forehead. He was in pain.

A teenage girl in her high school soccer uniform was sitting in a wheelchair, crying aloud about the fact that she would never get to play for the U.S. Women's team in the World Cup. She sobbed as she stared down at her leg, wishing that it wasn't broken.

I've always hated hospitals. There's a scent or a feel about them that just makes me uneasy. The unsure feeling that you get when you don't know if the person you are visiting is going to make it out grows inside my stomach every time I enter one.

Chris has always been allergic to bee stings. One summer I had to drive him to the hospital three times because he refused to carry an epinephrine needle with him. It seemed that the reaction happened quicker each time, and the trip to the hospital became an intense race against the clock, as his throat started to close up, and his eyes would swell shut. Every time I thought I was going to lose him.

Johnson came over and sat down next to me. I could see that he was fuming. I would be too if I was trying to find answers and was being cut off any time I tried.

"What the fuck is wrong with these people?" he asked me, shaking his head, as if he had come up with an answer to his own question.

"How long?" I asked.

"Fuck, I don't know," he said. "I just want to see my dad."

He lowered his head and closed his eyes. He violently shook his knee with nervous unease, hoping that everything would be okay but fearing what he knew was the probable conclusion to this story.

"Come on. Let's go smoke," I said, patting him on the shoulder.

I stood up and walked toward the door. Johnson stood up and reluctantly followed, eyeing the nurse's station on his way, hoping they would motion for him to come over.

We walked outside and stood in the entryway so that Johnson could see if the nurse called for him. I lit a cigarette and handed it to him. He took a drag and inhaled deeply. Then I pulled out another one and lit it for myself.

Johnson's eyes were laced with tears. Only his attitude about being strong and never crying was keeping him together. He believed in the façade of strength. If he appeared weak, that meant he was weak. If he appeared strong, that meant he was strong. He never showed weakness. It meant too much to him that he always appear to have it together, an unfortunate side effect of losing his mother at such a young age.

He didn't want to talk. I'm sure it was for fear of letting go, so we just sat in silence. He had dark stress rings beneath his eyes, and his face was flushed with confusion.

A man, probably in his mid-40s, with salt and pepper hair and a thin mustache, walked by us at that moment. He was holding the hand of a toe-headed little girl that appeared to be about eight.

"If you keep smoking," said the little girl, "you'll end up in here too."

"Fuck off," Johnson said, glaring at her with rage in his eyes.

"Really, kid?" I asked quietly, amazed Johnson would take his aggression out on a child.

The father stopped and turned around, equally upset, probably about someone in the hospital as well as Johnson's comment.

"Excuse me?" the man asked, letting go of his daughter's hand and stepping around to come to her defense.

Johnson flicked his cigarette into the ambulance roundabout and stared the man down, beckoning with his hands for him to come closer.

"Son, I think you need to learn some restraint," the man said.

"You going to teach it to me, old man?" Johnson asked.

The older man started to push up his sleeves, instructing his daughter to go inside.

"Hey!" I shouted and stepped in-between them. I pointed a single finger directly into Johnson's face. "Johnson, no!"

I looked Johnson in the eye and mouthed the words "calm down."

"Sir?" I said, turning and looking at the gentleman. "Go inside with your daughter. I apologize for this, but it would probably be best if you just went inside."

"You need to control your friend," he said, looking at me.

Johnson lunged at him shouting, "I don't need anyone to control me."

I managed to hold him back, but it took all of my might.

"Sir, be smart and go inside. It's a hospital," I said, restraining Johnson while staring at the man. "Everyone's a little on edge. You should be with your daughter right now, not out here with us."

"Look, young man" he began, condescension dripping from his tone as though he knew anything about Johnson's situation or mine.

"Now!" I screamed, cutting him off, pointing to the entrance.

He looked kind of stunned, but he shook it off quickly and finally walked inside. I turned my attention back to Johnson, who was pacing angrily up and down the sidewalk.

"Johnson, calm down."

He stopped pacing and took a deep breath.

"I'm sorry. That was, admittedly, out of line."

"Just breathe," I said. "Don't worry about it, just try to calm down".

He sat on a ledge that was neatly decorated with flowers and bushes in an unsuccessful attempt to make the hospital a cheerier place and took a few deep breaths.

"Feel better?" I asked.

He nodded and took a few more breaths. "A little out of control," he said, shaking his head again.

The nurse from the front desk quickly walked to the front door, peeking her head outside.

"Mr. McNamara," she called out to Johnson, "you can see him now."

Johnson's face turned bright red again, and his breathing became short and choppy.

"Come on," I said as I patted him on the back and nudged him through the doors.

The nurse led us to the entrance of the ER, punched in her code, and then let Johnson through.

"I'm sorry, sir," she said to me, "but you'll have to wait out here."

Johnson just looked at her and shook his head.

"No," he said. "I need him to come in with me."

"I'm sorry, but family members are the only ones allowed in," she said.

"He is family. He's my brother," Johnson argued.

The nurse looked down at her clipboard and shook her head. "He's not listed here so he can't come in."

"Look, I don't care what the fu…" Johnson started to say, but I cut him off with a hand on his shoulder.

"It's all good, man," I said. "I'll stay out here. You go see your dad."

Johnson nodded and then followed the Nurse Ratchett wannabe in through the doors. I walked over to the front desk and smiled at the duty nurse behind it.

"Can I help you?" she asked.

"Do you have a pen?" I asked in return.

She reached into her front pocket and handed me a black pen. I took it and smiled at her again.

"Yes?" she asked.

"How about some paper?" I asked, flashing my friendliest, most endearing smile.

She sighed, pulled a blank sheet of paper from the printer tray, and handed it to me.

"Thank you so much," I said.

"Mmm-hmm," she hummed through closed lips, sending a cold chill down my spine.

That is by far one of my worst pet peeves. How much extra effort does it take to say "No problem" or "You're welcome"? Hell, just a "Welcome" would suffice. I gritted my teeth and walked away.

I sat down and looked around the waiting room. The soccer player was still there, staring down at her ankle. The young boy was gone, along with his mother. In place of the boy and his mother, an older man, late 60s or so, with an oxygen tank, sat staring at the news on TV. Occasionally, he muttered to himself about something he'd just seen or heard.

God, I hate hospitals.

I looked down at the paper that the nurse had handed me and started writing:

> The world is dead,
> spinning out of habit.
> Life has ceased
> as I stop to breathe.
> Tears of the persecuted
> wash the blood
> from the hands of innocence
> for the other problems
> point the finger
> forgetting to turn it around.
> See sunlight fade into night
> as our souls become deadened
> as our medication
> takes away our personalities
> creating new ones.
> We don't know who we are.
> Too afraid to be ourselves,
> we run away with our hope.
> Finding life to be bland,
> we die.
> But we all stop to breathe

I put the pen down, folded up the paper and stuck it back in my pocket. I watched as the soccer girl got wheeled in through the double doors. Her mom was walking behind her, her face frozen in horror, as though she were watching her daughter enter the death chamber.

I leaned back in the chair, waiting for Johnson to come out, not knowing how long this would take. If Bill was on his deathbed, I don't know how long I would sit in the room with him. Maybe only for a few minutes, possibly all night. I was prepared to be there until the sun came up or even longer.

I watched as the older man with the oxygen tank got wheeled to the back, and a whole new cast of characters waiting to see the doctors took the place of the ones I had been observing since I arrived. My eyelids started to grow heavy as the alcohol I drank began to wear off and I was suddenly able to find the plastic chair just comfortable enough to lean my head back and fall asleep.

I was awakened a short time later when an alarm rang out in the waiting room area. My eyes snapped open as the nurse at the front desk fervently stood, grabbing the phone. She was screaming into the receiver in what sounded like Greek but was more than likely just anxious nerves.

That was when Johnson came bursting through the double doors, sprinting out through the lobby toward the exit. Three security guards were close behind him, yelling at him to stop.

"That can't be good," I said quietly to myself as I watched him run out the exit toward the night-covered streets of the city.

I sat in my chair, head pointed toward the floor, hoping that soon I'd be able to sneak out unnoticed so that I could go and find Johnson.

Less than a minute later, I was staring at three sets of feet.

I looked up, and found myself staring at the front desk nurse, a doctor, and a security guard.

"Hi," I said, giving them my best smile.

Their faces remained grim as they stared down at me over their noses.

"Where did your friend go?" asked the security guard, trying to intimidate me by tapping lightly on the black Chrised grip of his revolver.

"Who?" I asked with as much disdain I could muster.

"The man you came in with," said the nurse.

"Nurse Ratchett," said the security guard, "please allow me to handle this."

I laughed and said, "Your name is really Nurse Ratchett?"

All three of them glared at me.

"You know, the book? Ken Kesey? The Jack Nicholson movie?" I asked, but their expressions didn't change. "But you probably get that a lot."

I cleared my throat and tried to wipe the smile from my face.

"Son, this is serious," the guard said. "Where did he go?"

"Back to see his dad," I said, pointing at the double doors that I'd just seen them and Johnson sprint from only moments before.

"Didn't you just see him come running out of there?" he asked.

"No, Sir," I said as innocently as I could. "I didn't see that at all. I was asleep."

The doctor shook his head and sat down next to me.

"What's your name, son?" he asked.

"Jeremy Corso," I said, pulling the obscure beat poet's name off the top of my head.

"Jeremy," said the doctor, "your friend did something very bad, and we need to find him."

"Well, I'm sorry, Dr..." I began.

"Bruce Weigle," he said, looking at me with a knowing smile.

I looked at him, nodded and returned the smile.

"Now that we both know we're lying to each other," I said, "how about a little truth telling."

"What a novel idea," said Nurse Ratchett.

"Here's a novel for you," I said, sticking up my middle finger and looking into her dark, evil eyes.

"Jeremy," said Dr. Weigle, "this is you and I talking. Nurse Ratchett, can you please assume your position at the front desk?"

She scowled and stormed away.

"Now, Jeremy," he continued. "We need to know, where did he go?"

"What did he do?" I asked.

"You know that's confidential," he said.

"Gee, Bruce," I said, "I don't really remember walking in here with anybody.

"Son," the security guard again, still trying to intimidate me, "we need for you to cooperate, or we'll have you arrested."

"For what?" I laughed. "I'm just sitting here."

"Trespassing," he said.

"Okay. Ask me to leave and I will," I countered.

The guard just glared at me.

"George," said Dr. Weigle, "please go away. Jeremy, we need your help."

"You're not getting it without telling me what he did," I said.

Bruce sighed, then leaned in close.

"He unplugged his father's respirator and ripped out his IV," he said.

"Did he die?"

"No," he said, "he will. But...that's not your friend's fault."

"Then why do you need him?" I asked.

"He still attempted murder, Jeremy."

I could only nod.

"Alright, Bruce. I'll tell you what," I said. "I'll find him, and have him turn himself in on Tuesday."

"Why Tuesday?"

"'Cause," I said, "that's when the rest of my world falls apart."

"If I say no?"

"You don't really have a choice, Bruce. I'm walking out of here right now," I said, standing up, "and I can't be arrested for anything. But you have my word. He'll turn himself in."

Bruce nodded, and I turned and walked toward the front doors.

"Jeremy," he called. "Huge fan of your work, by the way."

I waved my hand in the air without looking back.

"Yours too, Bruce," I said as the front doors slid open.

XXIII.

It's a good thing that humans are creatures of habit, I thought, as I pulled into the parking lot of the Battlefield. I laughed thinking about Johnson's pending attempted murder charge, and now we were both committing a federal crime by entering the Battlefield at night. I hoped that if we got caught they wouldn't take that crime as seriously as they always threatened they would.

I got out of my car and started walking toward a lone tree that stood in the middle of a field. It didn't appear to be special or different from any of the other trees peppered across the battlefield. But for us, and probably a select few others, this tree was very special. Its branches reached out away from the trunk, then hung low and reached down, close to the ground. The way they had grown had left an open area near the trunk that was sheltered from the outside world by the branches. This became a small bastion from a world that was always pushing, pushing, pushing, and never seemed to give. It was where we used to come and sit whenever we were upset about anything. I knew that Johnson had been pushed to come here.

I pushed back the hanging branches and walked into the clearing. Johnson was leaning against the trunk, staring upward into the maze of branches and leaves, through small openings that pointed outward, exposing the night sky. I sat down next to him just as he was lighting a cigarette.

"Did I ever tell you I lost my virginity under this tree?" he asked me.

"No," I said, lighting a cigarette as well. I looked around and tried to imagine what it would have been like to make love under the tree. Completely hidden from the outside world but still open and romantic. I was a little envious of him. "Nice place for the first time."

"Yeah," he nodded. "To Julie Johnson. We always thought it was funny, that we both lost our virginities to Johnsons."

He chuckled slightly as the memory of Julie crossed his mind, and a wispy smile lingered on his lips.

"What happened?"

"I was upset, missed my mom–she was the one that showed me this tree," he said. He was staring at nothing in particular as he remembered. His eyes pointed toward leaves hanging from branches, but they weren't where we were. They were far off, in another time, another life for him. "I think it happened partially because she wanted me to feel better. Partially because she didn't want to be a virgin anymore."

He smiled again. If anyone were to see him at this moment, they would have no idea that he had recently tried to kill his father, and was currently running from the police. They would think he was just another guy reminiscing. He looked peaceful, at ease with everything in his life, just trying to figure out what he had to do next to live a life that made him feel good.

"We made love many times, right here in this spot," he said, motioning his hand over the ground next to him. "It was the best afternoon of my life."

"I meant, what happened to her?"

The smile left Johnson's face, and a look of contempt and anger took its place.

"Oh. My dad got drunk one night and came onto her," he said and then paused. "Somewhat forcibly. She never wanted to talk to him again. Which meant she never wanted to talk to me again either."

"I'm sorry, man," I said.

"I think that's why I always come here when I'm upset. It was such a perfect day, a perfect moment, a perfect girl. God, I really loved her," he said. Again, I watched as tears welled up in his eyes, and he blinked them away. "I mean...it was fucking real. I didn't date for years after that. Not until I could lie well enough to convince girls that my dad was dead."

"Pretty soon, it won't be a lie," I said.

Johnson looked at me. His eyes grew wide with shock.

"Pretty soon?" His voice was choppy and broken. Suddenly the gravity of what he had done started to sink in. The look of ease and relaxation that was on his face moments ago was completely gone.

"He didn't die, when you did...what you did," I said, knowing that the knowledge of failing at killing his father would be worse than the thought that he had.

He lowered his head and pounded his fist against the ground with such force I thought he could have broken his wrist.

"Will that bastard ever die?" he screamed.

"Why did you try to kill him?"

He shook his head and looked away. Through nights and days of what I could only imagine was constant hatred and doubt, Johnson had finally broken. His world had fractured and with it, the last thing that kept Johnson sane. He was shutting down, retreating to somewhere deep inside, searching his soul for the value of life.

We sat in silence for a long time, looking out toward where the horizon would be if the tree branches didn't shroud the view. I knew he needed to open up and talk about it or he would become a shell of the man he had become. I also knew that sometimes people just needed to think for a minute and sort their thoughts before committing to any real emotion.

"Hey," I asked again, after more than enough time had passed, "why did you try to kill your dad?"

His head whipped around.

"Because he fucking killed my mom!" he screamed.

"Oh," I said, stunned. "He finally admitted it today?"

"Like I was going to fucking forgive him, just because he's dying," he said, his voice growing with anger as he talked. "Fuck that! He killed my mom, lied about it for years, made me move away from my friends, made me an outcast for so long, and caused me to lose my first love. And I'm just supposed to forgive him, just because he's dying? It is my life that he fucked up, not his. His was already fucked."

"Did you really want to kill him though?"

"It would've been fair," he said coldly, flicking his cigarette and lighting a new one. "It would have been just."

"But then, you wouldn't have been any better than him."

"I would've felt redemption," he said. "Not the guilt that plagued him his whole life."

"It wouldn't matter in the eyes of anyone else," I said. "You'd still be a murderer. And then you would have to deal with the consequences."

"Even in your eyes?" he asked, looking at me for support, for justification.

"Johnson, I can understand when a wife kills her abusive husband, or a father kills a man that violated his child, or why you would want to kill your dad," I said. "But, they're still murderers, just like you would be, as far as I'm concerned, as far as the world's concerned. I can understand the motive, but it doesn't change how you would be seen. Justifiable homicide is still homicide."

Johnson lowered his head again. I wanted to console him, but I only had more bad news for him.

"The hospital's pressing charges. There's going to be a warrant out for your arrest."

Johnson laughed.

"For what?" he asked, incredulous. "He didn't even die."

"My bet would be *attempted* murder."

"That's fucking beautiful," he said, exasperated now. "The man kills my mother in a drunken haze of anger and impatience. Then the guilt causes him to drink himself even farther into alcoholism. Then he gets cirrhosis, hepatitis C, and surprisingly they won't give him a transplant because he can't stop drinking, and now as his liver is finally failing and he wants redemption for the mistakes he made in life, he admits that he murdered someone so many years ago. I shut off his machines so he would stop getting any sort of reprieve, so he could feel everything happening to him in his last few minutes, and I'm going to end up getting punished for his actions. Just fucking beautiful."

"Yeah," I said.

I could see that Johnson's mind was racing. His eyes darted from side to side as he tried to cope. The one thing that he needed, he had received, but unlike Chris, his came with a new set of problems, new issues that he had to work out. Only time would heal the newly administered wounds of torment, but time would not be kind in the healing process.

"You know what the real bitch of it is, man?" he asked.

I looked at him and shook my head.

"That night," he said, "the night that my mom died. I wasn't even at the house. I was staying at a friend's for my first sleepover."

He lowered his head, and I heard a slight quiver leave his mouth.

"I never got a chance to tell my mom that I loved her before she died," he continued. "What if I never begged to go to that sleepover? Would I still have her here with me? How different would my life be if I had never wanted to go as bad as I did? All I've ever wanted was to tell her that I love her one more time."

Years of bottled up emotion and pent up frustration started to cross his face. I knew that no matter what had happened that night, Johnson's life wouldn't be that different. What happened probably would have happened another night or another night or another when he wasn't around, and the same questions would be running through his brain, wondering how he could have done something different. There would never be any real answers though, only more questions. And though the story would be different, and the cast of characters slightly skewed, the ending would always be the same. He and I would still be sitting here, him asking me what if, in a never-ending cycle of hypothetical situations that would only lead him to more questions without any answers.

"And because of him," he said, "I lost my friends at a young age and was forced to move somewhere, surrounded by rumors and hearsay that made me and him pariahs in a small, fucked up town. I had nothing in my life but him. He took everything from me before I even had a chance to realize that I had lost anything."

The sun started to rise. Light crept through slight openings in the branches and the small area of openness that rested between the branches and the ground splaying out around us. Johnson looked at the ground and stubbed out his cigarette, shaking his head.

"And now, I'm never going to see him again because I'll get arrested if I go there," he said, pounding his fist into the soft, dew-soaked ground. "And I can't even tell him that I fucking hate him."

"I'm pretty sure that trying to kill him gave a good clue," I said, hoping to bring some levity to the situation, cringing at my awkward timing.

"But," he stopped, staring at the ground, either ignoring my last sentence or so lost in his own train of thought he didn't hear me. "I'll never get to tell him thank you or how much I love him either."

He turned and looked at me. For the first time since I met him, he seemed young. Young and scared. As actuality finally set in, he knew there was nothing else for him to do. He couldn't hide from himself anymore. The walls Johnson had built that helped him hold back all of his emotion and wear that façade of strength, they all broke down and he started to cry.

His tears turned into sobs as he leaned his head to my shoulder, and I put my arm around him, consoling my old friend in the darkest moment of his already dark life. I knew I had to be strong for him so I blinked back the tears caused by a sorrow that only comes when you see the eternal distress of a friend or family member. To me, Johnson was both.

"It's going to be okay," I said, knowing that only these words were appropriate at a time like this. Even with all the doubt that circled my own head about what his future might bring. "It's going to be okay."

Johnson cried. He cried with the sadness that only decades of hiding pain could bring. Everything that he had bottled up, everything that he had chalked up to explanations of fate and luck and bad timing, came pouring over the top as the weight of what real life can do to one person entered the depths of Johnson's soul and displaced where he had hidden reality. In this time of suffering, questioning, and eye opening, Johnson was only able to say one thing over and over: "I fucked this up."

XXIV.

Johnson crashed out on Rich's couch. He wanted to go back to his house to pick up some clothes, and I had to sway him from the idea for fear the police would be there, waiting for him.

It didn't take very long for him to fall asleep, but I sat at the table wide awake, thinking. I picked up a pen and started scribbling on a napkin that was lying next to my arm:

The end has come.
It's all up for silent auction.
I don't care for it anymore.
There's no getting over it.
The brow is furrowed,
Eyes pointed in rage,
Pulse is raised.
The bottle smashed.
It's all a bunch of broken pieces.
The temperature drops.
Rain stings bare skin.
They all feel like tears,
but freeze before

they hit the ground.
Cars sound like kittens
until they collide
with other felines.
The windshield is now
broken pieces.
Rules of attraction
apply to no one.
Everything is so typical.
No one really knows anyone.
Everyone is made of porcelain,
we all smash someday.
We dream of crashing,
long to relapse.
We are nothing more than
broken pieces,
pieces that will never be picked up.

I put the pen down and looked back at Johnson. He began to snore lightly. I lit a cigarette and started to cry. I cried for my friend, and I cried for the life that he had been hiding from since he was a little kid, forced to always question who he was, where he belonged. I cried because I was lucky to not have his life, but wished that I could have lived it for him so he wouldn't have to deal with the pain that he was now living with. I cried because at that moment, I didn't know what else to do to or how to fix anything in the world around me.

I almost wished I still used so I could numb the sadness that I felt throughout my body.

I was still awake when Rich came out of his room at 11. He walked into the living room rubbing his eyes and sat down across from me at the table. He looked first at Johnson lying on the couch and then at me.

"God, you look like shit, Kid," he said, lighting a cigarette.

I replied with an inaudible grunt.

"How was last night?" he asked.

Again, the grunt.

"That good, huh?"

I nodded.

"How's Johnson's dad?"

I looked at him and slowly shook my head.

"How's he taking it?" he asked, nodding in Johnson's direction.

"Surprisingly well," I said, finally deciding to talk. I pulled a cigarette out and lit it. "But you might want him to tell you that story."

I walked into the kitchen and started a pot of coffee.

"Have you slept yet?" he called into the kitchen.

"No," I said, walking back into the living room, "I'll grab an hour or two later today."

"You know that's sexual harassment," Rich said with a smile.

"What?" The dumbfounded look I gave him made him smile even more.

"Never mind," he said, seeing that his attempt at humor had completely missed me.

I sat back down and looked around. "Where's Chris?"

"Left out of here with Kayla last night."

"No fucking way."

"No shit. After Johnson and you went to the hospital, Chris turned into every single character from his stories." Rich shook his head, dumbfounded. "He was charming, intelligent, quick thinking, funny. The transformation was fucking incredible."

"I knew he had it in him," I said, standing up to get coffee for the two of us, and he followed me into the kitchen. "I mean, how else do you get into relationships? You pick either one of his two relationships, and they're longer than all of mine put together. You have to be somewhat charming for that to happen."

"Or you just have to be able to bend backwards," he said.

I handed Rich his coffee and he took a sip. He gave me a look of pleasant surprise when he tasted it.

"How'd you make this taste good? This stuff is usually shit."

"I put some cinnamon in the filter," I said. "Figured that out around 6 this morning."

"Cinnamon," he said softly, nodding his head and staring amorously at his cup. Suddenly he snapped his head up and looked at me.

"What do we do today?" he asked.

"When was the last time you were at the coffee shop?" I asked, taking a sip of coffee.

I took a two-hour power nap after Johnson woke up while we waited for Chris.

When the four of us were all together we headed for the coffee shop, notebooks in hand, pens in pockets, and smiles on our faces. In my mind I've always pictured it like a movie—the four of us smiling, walking through the door in slow-motion, all of the customers and employees staring at us, mouths agape, as we walk up to the counter together, some instrumental song from the 70s playing over the loud speakers.

"My God," Nate, the owner of the coffee shop said. "I never thought the four of you would be back in here again."

Nate was an older gentleman, mid-40s or so. He had brown hair and a beard that was streaked with gray, no doubt a result of the stress from 14 adopted kids, not to mention memories of the Vietnam War.

We all said hi, and Nate made our drinks without us telling him what we wanted. After so many years, he still remembered my extra shot of espresso, Chris's extra squirt of mocha, and Johnson's caramel.

The four of us sat down at the table in the window and silently sipped our coffee. Piercing glances shot from each of us as we tried to find the words to describe what we were thinking. We all knew the reunion was drawing to a close.

"Goddamn," Rich said. "It's so much like the first time we got together again."

I smiled because it was true. There was something ominous to the atmosphere, something awkward and foreboding. It was as though we all knew this would be the last time we were at the coffee shop together.

"I can't believe you're leaving," Johnson said to Rich.

"I have to go find myself," Rich said. "I think I lost me a while ago. I miss having me around."

"It'll be a hell of an adventure," Chris said.

Rich nodded and took a sip of his coffee.

"I'll miss these times though," I said.

"They'll happen again," Rich said. "Hell, if Neal could get us all together on bad terms, it ought to be easy as shit next time around."

"So nobody go pissing anybody off," said Chris, sarcastically waving his finger in each of our directions.

"That means you, Neal," Johnson added, giving me a wink.

"No promises," I said,

"So what about you, Mr. Junior?" Rich asked. "What are you going to do?"

I'd been thinking about this a lot, but I still had no answers.

"You know, Mr. Stevens, I have no fucking idea. There are so many pros and cons to both sides of the decision, I really don't know what the better choice is."

Chris started laughing. He laughed so hard that he was having trouble breathing. We all stared at him as he gasped for breath between guffaws.

"What the fuck is your issue?" Johnson asked him.

"Allow me to explain," he said, after regaining his composure. Then he looked at me and smiled. "Neal is an adventurer. Think about it. What hasn't he done? Where hasn't he gone? He's been across the country more times than I've been to the beach. He's written articles, stories, and poems about places and things that I can only dream of. He's run the gamut of prep to junkie to beat to unnamed category that he's the only member of. He's not afraid to try anything or do anything. And that's made him the man he is today."

Rich and Johnson nodded in agreement. I shook my head as Chris tried to analyze me again. He may know me better than anyone, but he never could guess what I was going to do next.

"But," he continued, "throughout it all, he's remained unavailable. Detached from friends and family. I'm not saying you don't love us, Neal. I know you'd do anything for us and never complain once."

I nodded and looked around the circle. There was so much truth in that statement. If Johnson had asked me to pull the plug the night before, I would have without thinking about it. If Chris needed me to come back for any reason, it wouldn't matter where in the world I was, I would get back to help him immediately. And for Rich, I would go to the ends of the earth to make sure he stayed clean. I loved these guys. They were the only real family I ever knew.

"I'll admit, I wish I could be him sometimes," he said, addressing the others, "and do the things he does. At times I'm jealous. But then I remember, there's one adventure I've embarked on that he never has. I'm sure it's the fact that the opportunity never came up or that he's always managed to escape before facing it head on."

A smile crossed his face as he looked at me.

"I'm talking about love," he went on, "and it's the only trip we've taken that he never has. He'll stay 'cause he needs to fall. He wants to fall. He'll stay 'cause he's already fallen...in love with Meagan."

Johnson and Rich looked at me, waiting for my response to Chris's opinionated rant.

"Did you just come up with that?" I asked.

Chris nodded.

"It was good," I said. "Misguided, but good."

"What?" he asked.

"I'm fucking terrified of every single thing I do," I said, with a slightly arrogant grin.

"But you still do it," he said.

"Only because I tell you guys that I'm going to. I tell you guys what I'm going to do because I'm scared to do it," I said.

"'Service Boy' was a cry for help," said Johnson.

I snapped my fingers and pointed at him.

"Exactly. I want to be brave, but I'm afraid of just about everything. I want to fall in love, but I've seen all of you get your hearts broken, especially you, Chris," I said, now pointing at him, "and that scares the living shit out of me. I don't know if I could handle it as well as you do. And you don't handle it well at all."

"That's half of what makes us who we are," said Rich. "How we handle ourselves when heartbroken. You're a strong person, Neal."

"I appreciate that," I said, "but I'm not. I don't persevere like you think I do."

"Aside from being modest," Johnson said, "you're avoiding the issue. Have you tripped or not?"

I looked at him and laughed.

XXV.

We left the coffee shop and headed out. None of us knew where we were going that night. We just knew that we were going together.

I called Meagan and let her know that I was going out with the guys and that I would see her tomorrow. She said she couldn't wait. My mind exploded with possibilities of what might happen when I saw her.

The four of us went to the bar, for what was supposed to be a few drinks but ended up turning into a drunken festival of ideas and concepts being tossed back and forth in attempts to build and improve on what we already hoped would be nothing less than fantastic.

"I have an idea," Chris said after throwing back a shot of Jack Black and taking a sip of his beer to chase it down. "A poetry book, where the reader makes all the choices."

"What do you mean?" I asked, almost choking on my beer as I tried to hold back the laughter. It seemed like an asinine idea the moment he said it.

"There are no separate titles," he said, "no breaks between the poems, they all run together, like a dream. But the reader can decide what one poem is. Maybe the whole book is a single poem, or maybe just one page, or a single line. It's completely up to the reader."

I looked at him, amazed that I actually liked the idea. It may have been the beer and shots that fueled my fondness, but I started to envision how I would do something in the same vein.

"That's a great fucking idea," I said. "You could write down anything but keep it as one common theme."

"I was thinking if you write it all as a dream, at the end you could have him wake up and answer his own questions," he said. "Or not, I guess, it would be up to you."

"Run with it," I said, "then let me read it, or e-mail me a copy, or whatever."

Chris took a slug from his beer and shook his head as he swallowed.

"No, I want you to write it," he said. "That's why I told you about it."

"I'm not doing your idea," I said. "That one's too good to steal."

"But you're a better poet," he insisted, pointing the neck of his beer bottle in my direction.

"No, I'm not. I just work on it more often," I said. "By the time you're done with this idea, you could be the best."

"Out of the four of us?" he asked, with a tone in his voice that screamed "yeah, right."

"Ever," I said, staring at him in the eyes. My face remained completely somber as I said it. He stared back at me, waiting, I'm sure, for me to give him some indication that I was joking or being sarcastic. But I wasn't. "Believe in your talent, Chris. You have more of it than I do."

"I know," Chris said, with a shrug that seemed to throw the comment off to the wayside. I looked at him, surprised that he would say something so arrogant and brazen. "I know that I am the most talented one here. I also know I've squandered my talent on drugs and drinking and doubt."

"I wouldn't say squandered," I said, but he held up a hand to cut me off.

"I want to write something excellent," he said, "something that will be remembered for generations. That parents will pass down to their kids, who will pass it down to their kids, who will pass it down to their kids. I want my name to be remembered by a larger group of people than the select few that find this thing that we do romantic or inspiring or whatever."

"I believe you could do it," I said, not knowing why something like widespread fame seemed so appealing to him. I preferred the solitary lifestyle of being able to go out without people hounding me for autographs or asking me about my next project. Chris, though, he always needed something that I never understood, a level of acceptance from everyone that fueled most of what he did. His desire to be liked bordered on the level of obsessive, but it was also what attracted so many to him.

"I've already started it," he said, interrupting my thought process. "Which is why I want you to write the poem. I even have the title for you."

"What's the title?"

"1 to Infinite," he said, smiling and sipping on his beer.

It was perfect. A riddle of a title that lets the reader know there are an endless amount of combinations for different poems in one book. I smiled and nodded my head.

"I love it," I said.

He raised his bottle to show his appreciation of my acceptance.

"What is this new thing you are working on?" I asked.

A slight smile crossed his face, and his eyes seemed to light up as he thought of the idea.

"It's something slightly outside of my wheelhouse," he said. "It's a kids' series."

I almost spit out the swallow of beer I was currently drinking. I looked at him with adulation. A slight amount of pinkish color came to his cheeks as he said the words. He seemed embarrassed by the idea, or at least by the idea that he would be the one writing it. Chris Franklyn, the former drug addict, the borderline alcoholic, the forever heartbroken, beaten man, wanted to write a kids' series.

"A kids' series?"

Chris laughed and nodded.

"Yeah," he said, slurring his speech slightly as he spoke. "About a boy named Mike and his teddy bear, Sebastian, and their adventures together trying to save the world of Bearlandia against the evil scarecrow, Upjack."

I nodded. I was never able to think about things the way that he could. When I wrote, I wrote about things that were real, that I had experienced, or could have seen happening in a real world. Chris had the ability to see a completely made up world in his mind and run with it. It was his ability to detach himself from reality that made him the more talented writer. I was slightly envious of him at that moment.

"I am going to have my hands kind of full with it," he said. "You know, creating a whole new world isn't as easy as one would think. Which is why I want you to write '1 to Infinite.'"

I put my hand out, and he lightly placed his against mine so they were resting against each other, palm to palm.

"2:30 a.m.," I said.

"2:30 a.m.," he repeated, smiling. "I can't wait to read it."

I laughed. "Neither can I."

Rich ran over to us in an overly excited state. "Neal," he screamed, "watch this!"

He grabbed the pen I had hanging from the neckline of my shirt and a bar napkin and started writing frantically. In less than a minute, he'd filled both sides of it.

"I can write again," he declared, holding up the napkin triumphantly like it was the Pulitzer Prize.

"Let's see how you did," I said, taking it from him. I read aloud:

> I may be drunk
> but I can think clearly.
> The mistakes I made
> are now so obvious,
> I was told to fear The Reaper
> but know to fear nothing
> as long as I have friends.

We're the voice of the revolution
spitting in the eye of conformity
we shall not be shackled
we found our own beat
that we never march in time to.
We live a life
that is anything but ordinary
and bask in our ideals.
People may question our morals
but we can still say
fuck you, let us be
let us live our life
we don't question you
please don't judge us.
We find redemption
in our own way.
Sorry if you disagree.
Don't be jealous
'cause we like to drink.

"The ending needs some work," Chris said.

"Fuck that!" Rich said. "No edits. It's how I felt at the time. It stays." He marched away, obviously proud of his re-found ability.

"That was really, really terrible," I said quietly after he left. "But I do like the idea of us being the voice of a revolution."

"And to think, you're the leader," Chris said. "How does that feel?"

"You tell me, Chris," I said, looking at him. "You've always been the leader. You're the reason we're here."

"You flatter me," he said, waving his hand in the air as though accepting a compliment from the royal family in an old movie. "I'll accept the compliment."

I put my hand on his shoulder and looked him square in the eyes. "Swear that you'll never let this die."

Chris finished his beer and looked at me.

"We'll never die, Neal," he said. "Not as long as people read."

I nodded and finished my beer. "C'mon, let's get Drunk Boy home."

XXVI.

Pull it out the pack
light it up
smoke it down
put it out.
The circle is there for life.
It doesn't hurt
as bad as you think.
The scab becomes raised
pull it off.
It won't bleed much.
Never forget.

As we put the last of Rich's thing in his car, the four of us shared a sense of accomplishment. It was the first time in years that we'd all been together to see one of our friends off, off to teach the truth he knew to others and to learn the truth that others know. I tossed the last bag in and slammed the trunk down.

"You're all set, Kid," I said, patting Rich on the arm. "You ready?"

He nodded as he stared at the license plate. I'm sure he was contemplating the next move–where he would be in the next few days, weeks, and months, until he found himself feeling like himself again.

"I hope we get to do this again," Chris said.

"It just sucks that this moment, and all the others that we've shared this week, will fade away like every other memory," Johnson said, shaking his head.

I looked at Chris who gave me a little smile and shrugged. I chuckled to myself.

"What?" Rich asked.

"Lift up your sleeve," I said. "You too, Johnson."

They lifted their sleeves up to their shoulders, and I took a look at them.

"Now, in this day and age, becoming blood brothers with anyone is really fucking dangerous," I said, pulling out my pack of cigarettes. I handed a cigarette to each of my friends. "But I know of something we can do that'll bind us the same way, without spreading whatever diseases you all may have picked up."

We all lit our cigarettes, and I pulled out a pen. On each person's left shoulder I put a small 'X' with a circle around it.

"I'm sure you can all figure out what we're about to do," I said.

Rich looked at his arm. "Is this going to hurt?"

"Not as bad as you think it will," Chris said. "The trick is to try and get angry right before you do it. For some reason it helps numb the pain."

Rich nodded. "How many times have you all done this?"

"Five," Chris said.

"Seven," I said.

"You have that many moments you wanted to remember that badly?" Johnson asked.

"Don't really have a choice now," I said. "That's why you have to make sure you really want to remember the moment. The reminder will be there forever."

Our cigarettes were almost down to the filters.

"You guys ready?" Chris asked, taking a deep breath.

We all nodded. Johnson and Rich had a slight amount of reluctance in their demeanor. At the same time, we all plunged the glowing cherries into our shoulders. The burning tobacco and nicotine dove into the flesh, eating through it like a parasite destroys its host. The pain made me feel alive, for a quick moment, and then the sorrow set in. A kind of sadness swept through my body, sadness that it takes something like a cigarette on skin to make me feel something real. This was a momentous occasion that would forever be remembered by me every time I ran my finger over the scar that would soon appear. Every time I took off my shirt or stood in front of the mirror after a shower, I would see a reminder of the new birth for the four of us. I promised myself that nothing would ever be this important again, and thus I would never need to burn myself again. It was time I allowed myself to feel something that wasn't caused by pain.

"Hold it there until it's out," I warned through clenched teeth.

We pulled the stamped out cigarettes away from our arms. We each had a small circle, where the skin had melted and folded over. They were all red, with hints of pink, and some black specks scattered through them from the ash. Slowly they would swell, grow and morph into their individual scars. Made the same way but each with their own distinct characteristics.

"You lying motherfuckers," Johnson exclaimed, rubbing his arm lightly. "That hurt like hell."

"Sissy," I said, flicking my cigarette into the street.

"Anyone who saw us do that probably thinks we're insane," Rich said, also rubbing his arm.

"Fuck 'em," I said. I looked up and noticed the old blue haired lady who always seemed to be standing out on her patio scowling at us. I had a good laugh on the inside.

Checking out the newly formed wound on my arm, I brushed away the loose ash that sat in the crevasses and valleys. A certain joy passed over me as I thought about the reasoning behind what we had just done. It was symbolic of everything that was us. Forever we would remember each other in this moment, through pain. I slowly looked over the faces of Chris, Johnson, and Rich. Each one was smiling ear to ear, as was I, and we laughed and joked about the past week. The disputes and arguments of the past were exactly that. We each had brand new life injected into us. Life that was infected with something that none of us had ever really experienced before.

It was a life with the possibility of happiness.

The moment of camaraderie and bonding passed and was replaced with awkwardness. No one knew what to say. We stood around shuffling our feet, clearing our throats, rubbing our arms, running our fingers over our hair, and waiting for someone to say the first goodbye. We'd done this many times before, but the moment never changed. No one ever wanted to say it.

"Alright," Rich said. "I've got to go, before I decide not to."

Chris reached out and took Rich's hand. Rich pulled him in and gave him a hug.

"Stay clean, Brother," Chris said.

"You too," said Rich.

They patted each other on the backs and let go. Rich turned to Johnson, who avoided the handshake and went straight to the hug.

"Be good out there," Johnson said.

"I'm never that good," he said.

They let go and Rich turned to me.

"My Brother," he said, "I can never thank you enough for the past week."

"And you know that you never have to, even once," I said.

"What's next for you?" he asked.

"I think," I said, looking around, "it might be time for me to move on again."

"So that's it?" he asked. "Neal is running away again?"

"Neal doesn't know what he's doing," I said, "but I'm doing what I think is the right thing for me right now."

"Where you going to head first?" he asked.

I shrugged. I hadn't given it any amount of thought. There was an infinite number of possibilities out there—where I could go, what stories I could live. A blank piece of paper made up my future, and it was up to me to write the adventure that would fill it.

"I have no idea," I said.

"You want to go with me?" he asked, pointing to the empty passenger seat.

I shook my head.

"I've done the adventure that you are about to embark on," I said. "This is your adventure, and you need to write it as you see it. I'd only hinder you. I need my own adventure."

"So then, this is goodbye," he said.

"Goodbye is final," I said. "This is, until we come back around again, or until we meet up again. This better not be goodbye."

He hugged me and I hugged him back.

"We've done this too much this week," I said as our embrace lingered on.

"We definitely have," he said. "When we get together again, let's try not to do this as much."

"Deal."

We took a step back. He nodded at each of us and got into his car.

I walked over to where Johnson and Chris were standing as Rich pulled out of his parking space and headed out of the lot. He stuck his arm out the window, waving as he turned onto the main road, on his way toward his grand adventure.

"What now?" Chris asked.

I shrugged and Johnson shook his head.

"This is going to be it," Chris said. "Isn't it?"

Chris was a constant worrier. It was practically an "itis" with him. He feared the worst in nearly every situation he was confronted with. With all of the work we had done repairing relationships he didn't want this past week to be lost in a sea of forgotten memories and anecdotes we would tell to people we randomly met in varying bars years later.

"Don't worry, Kid," I said. "The four of us will always be together from now on."

"What are you talking about?" Chris asked. "Rich just left."

"I'm not talking about just in the physical sense of the word," I explained. "This also includes the emotional sense."

Johnson pulled out a cigarette and nodded as he lit it.

"Neal's right," he said. "The funny thing about life is how funny it can be."

Chris chuckled to himself as he pulled a cigarette out and lit it as well.

"That's a pretty fucking terrible line," he said exhaling the smoke from his lungs.

"But it's true," I said. "Think about it. If you had asked me last week if Johnson and I would ever speak again I would have unequivocally said no. Now the two of us are closer than we may have ever been."

Johnson nodded.

"And if you had asked me what I would predict in your future," he said to Chris, "you would have eventually overdosed, or at the very least ended up someone's bitch in prison."

Chris and I both chuckled.

"It's true," Chris said. "I am too pretty for prison."

"We all like to think that," Johnson said.

I chuckled.

"Johnson would have gotten the shit kicked out of him, probably multiple times," I said. "By someone other than me."

"Hey," Johnson said, pointing an angry finger at me. "I'll just get Chris to kick the shit out of you."

I laughed and gave him an apologetic wink.

"Rich would have been in jail for some crazy attempt at getting to the next big high," I went on. "Or he would have just faded away into nothing."

"He truly was on a pathway to oblivion," Chris said.

"I'm surprised we all got a chance to get together again in a situation that wasn't his funeral," Johnson said, taking a slow drag off his cigarette.

"Exactly!" I exclaimed. "Now all of us have the opportunity to make something of ourselves, and that is due to the fact that we were there to help each other out in our greatest time of need."

"That's what you do for your best friends," Chris said.

"Even when you all hate each other," Johnson quipped.

"And because of that, the four of us will never leave each other," I said. "There will forever be a little piece of each of you in me, just as I like to think that there is a little piece of me in each of you."

Both Chris and Johnson nodded with smiles across their faces. Each one of us suddenly saw possibilities forming in the future that could be tasted, and they tasted sweet.

Life was at our fingertips, waiting for us to grab on and make it ours. We all knew our paths were separating at this moment, but none of us knew where he was going. I didn't want to leave them, but I knew there was one more thing I had to do before I left.

I looked at Chris and Johnson and started to say something, but I couldn't find the right words to say.

"Don't worry, Kid," Chris said. "Go do what you have to do."

Johnson nodded and smiled. "Good luck, Neal."

I looked at them, and even though I was filled with excitement, I knew I had to say something before I left, to thank them for everything, to express my gratitude for their friendship and their loyalty and their support. I wanted it to be poetic and perfect for the moment. I wanted it to be something that they could quote in stories and poems they wrote. I wanted it to be epic.

I opened my mouth and said the only words that came to mind.

"I love you guys."

I jumped into my car, turning the ignition, feeling the vibration of the seat as the engine roared to life. I looked out my driver side window at Chris and Johnson watching me with smiles on their faces.

Chris nodded at me, telling me to roll my window down.

"Hey Neal," he said. "I can't wait for the next crisis that gets the four of us together again. Even though it was emotionally draining, this was the best week of my life."

Johnson nodded, his tell tale smirk plastered on his face.

I smiled. It was not the most poetic thing he ever said but probably the most honest. I couldn't have agreed with him more.

I put the gearshift into drive and pulled out of the parking lot. Until the car runs out of gas, I would drive onward, waiting to find my next great adventure

Diary Entry XVI:

Dear Jack,

 I'm not sure how long it's been for every day feels like an eternity. It's been a month and a half now since I used anything. Today I'm in Florida, tomorrow, it's up to the whim of the road. I can do whatever I want again, and I even remember it clearly the next day. The fresh ocean air revives a spark that's grown dim over the past few years. I remember the small things in life, the things that really matter. The other day I walked past a girl that smelled so incredible. It made my entire day better than any dream.

 Chris is back at his old job, but the last time we talked, he said all of his free time is being spent on a book. He said it's some fantasy kids' book about a kid and his teddy bear. Only Chris is crazy enough to write something like that. He and Kayla, a girl he met at my house a while back, have been dating for some time now. He says that he's pleasure delaying with her. But we all know that she doesn't want to give him any until she's certain their relationship is not just about sex. Oh yeah, he's also on the same train I am. He hasn't used since we all parted ways.

 Johnson's back to his old self. His dad refused to press charges against him so the case was null and void. He went to the funeral a few weeks after I left. He said that not many people showed up. I think it gave him some sense of closure. When I talked to him about it he said that he got to say, "thank you," or something. I wasn't really sure what he was talking about. He is spending some time in the northwest, last I heard from him he was in Seattle staying with Chris's uncle for a few weeks trying to figure shit out. I may have to swing up there sometime soon to see what he is up to.

And Neal, my God, his is a story that is so laden with clichés I can't even bring myself to write it here for fear of thinking one day I made it all up. That man lives on the edge of a world that only he sees, and good for him. To be able to live like him would be a dream that only a certain type subconscious could possibly fathom.

I wish the four of us were out here together, but we are all off on our own adventures. And we can't end them yet, not until they are completed.

It's amazing how life can suddenly change. I never understood how fragile it all is, then it hit me. I realized that life is what you make it. If you want it to be shit, or if you don't care if it's good, it'll be shit. If you desire it to be grand, you can make it more beautiful than the moon at 2:30 a.m.

Jack, right now, I want it to be better than grand. And fucking life is good. You have to savor every minute of it. Every moment that passes is another minute that you never get back. There isn't another chance at it. Speaking of which, a second in a mini-skirt, halter-top, with a lip ring and a few provocative tattoos just walked by, and this moment shall not slip through the cracks.

Goodbye, my Brother, talk to you soon.

From one subterranean to another,
Rich Stevens

Epilogue

The night Rich left I filled my car with gas, made sure I had all of the stuff I would need for my next adventure, then went to Meagan's house. She didn't know I was coming over, and I felt a little bad about not giving her any warning. But I had to see her.

I got out of the car and ran up to the door. I pounded on the window, over and over, until I saw her peek out. She swung open the door and stepped out.

"Neal. What the…" she started to say, but I pulled her in and kissed her before she could finish. She resisted for a second then wrapped her arms around my neck and kissed me back.

"You've got to stop doing that," she said when we'd finished. "What was that for?"

"I've been thinking about doing that all day."

She kissed me lightly on the lips and then smiled. "What's up?" she asked.

"Rich left today," I said.

Her eyes went vacant. She feared what I was about to say. I knew what I had to do, what I had to say, but the fear of her response ate at my stomach causing a pain that shot through my body. I was not feeling my normal confident self. My palms were sweaty, and I was very aware of every movement I made.

"What's that mean?" she asked.

"I," I said and then stopped. I had no idea how to say what I wanted to say. I wanted the words to come to me easily, but they just weren't flowing.

Meagan looked at me, her eyes narrowed.

"I get it," she said. "Thank you for coming to tell me face to face. At least you aren't a coward."

She turned and started to walk back inside. I felt my opportunity passing me by. I had talked to so many women in my lifetime, most of whom I didn't care if they were there or not. This time I did care. I just wanted to say anything to keep her there, but I felt like I was choking.

"Wait," I said.

She stopped and turned around. Her arms were folded across her chest, and her blue eyes glared at me.

"I've," I said, pausing again as my stomach twisted from nervous energy. "I've never done this."

Meagan shook her head and spread her arms outward.

"I'm glad I could be your first."

I held my hands up defensively.

"No, wait," I said. "I have to figure out how to say what I need to say."

She crossed her arms once again. I could see that she was very annoyed with me.

"Take a chance with me," I blurted out, assuming that saying anything would be better than saying nothing.

"What?" she asked, breaking from her defensive stance.

"I want you to take a chance with me," I said again.

"How so?"

"Meagan, I feel like you and I are just at the beginning of what is supposed to happen with us," I said. "We have a story that we're supposed to live out." I closed my eyes and bit my lower lip. Terror went through my body. I wasn't sure how I would react if she said no. "Right now," I continued, "you and I are at the first page of what could be the beginning of a very short story or an epic adventure. It all depends on what you choose tonight."

"What do I have to choose?"

"You have to make the choice to come with me," I said.

I could see in her eyes that she was as afraid as I was about this conversation. Who could blame her? This was the most insane thing I had ever proposed, and I left my senior year of high school behind to drive across the country.

"I know that this is a risk," I said. "We hardly even know each other! Yet it feels like we know everything about each other. It was supposed to happen this way. This moment. This precise moment, we are faced with an option that we will be able to tell people about for the rest of our lives. I know it's terrifying, but when I look back on my life, I like the fact that I will be able to say that I took the chance and asked you to come with me."

My heart pounded. I could feel the pressure building behind my eyes. The tension I felt hung in the air like a man on the gallows, noose around his neck, waiting for the door to drop open, sending him to his fate. The only thing left for him was the option of saying his last words.

"I want you to come with me," I said, my hands soaked with sweat. "I want us to go out on the road and tell the story that is supposed to be told. So…when you look back on your life, will you be able to people that you had a guy ask you to go on the road with him or that you went out on the road with this guy you barely knew but felt like you knew everything about him?"

"What you're asking of me is crazy," she said.

"I know," I said, "but this could be the beginning of the greatest story of your life."

"It could also be the worst."

"Do you think so?"

She looked down and closed her eyes. She shuffled her feet nervously. I could see her mind racing. I knew that she was realizing it was more insane for her to say yes than no to me, but I was almost positive that she was considering the innate benefits and joy that could be achieved if she said yes.

"How am I supposed to say yes to this?" she asked.

"By opening your mouth and saying three little letters in a row."

I could hear my heart beating in my ears, like it was bursting out of my chest. I nervously chewed on my lower lip, fighting the urge to light a cigarette, walk away, rescind my offer, and decide to stay to be with her. Anxious and afraid, I waited with bated breath as the moment, which could have been one second but which felt like an eternity, passed.

She looked up at me, her blue eyes sparkling from the streetlight. Her face was somber, and I could feel my heart sinking farther and farther into my chest as she slowly opened her mouth. I couldn't even breathe as she started to speak.

"Neal," she said.

In that moment I had lost every ounce of fear that hung on my body only moments before. Suddenly feeling weightless and alive, I floated as her lips moved, ever so delicately, and the word, "Yes," left her throat and danced through the air that rested between us landing in my ears, freeing me of every ounce of stress, worry, and apprehension that I had ever felt about anything that was not as important as that moment.

A blank slate was resting before us, stretching out as far as eternity. The infinite amount of options that I saw for myself, against all scientific and mathematical possibility, doubled. Every possible scenario that I played out in my mind became more enjoyable as I pictured what life would be like in the watercolor world of perfection that I painted in my head.

Even in the moment I was aware of the undeniable arrogance that I displayed in my own psyche. I knew that nothing ever works out the way you imagine it, and the future can't be envisioned in the mind of a lowly writer. The fantasy of perfection was one I had all the time, but I had never experienced it with another person in the scene. This perfection was the type of fantasy I had been missing out on for my life, one that I wanted to cling to until I realized that the fantasy was not reality.

I took her by the hand and walked her to my car—the chariot that would take us on the first of what would undoubtedly be many adventures. I chivalrously opened the door for her and let her in. She kissed me on the lips as she sat down. Like an excited teen on prom night, wondering if this would be the night that he would finally lose his virginity, I ran around to the other side, swung the door open and leapt into the driver's seat.

I leaned over and kissed her fully on the mouth, fueled by an amount of passion and a level of feeling that I had no concept of before this moment. In an unfettered moment of perfection that will never end since I was sure to memorize it from every angle, I realized that I was, in fact, happy.

The kiss ended, and the smile that was shining on my face told her the entire story.

She smiled too—her precious perfect smile, kissed her hand and lightly placed it against my cheek. I leaned into her hand, hoping that she would let it linger there for a moment longer, her touch sending waves of joy and excitement through my body.

"Oh, by the way," I said as I started the car, trying not to smile as goofily as I felt I was. "I wrote this for you."

I reached into my pocket and handed her a folded up piece of paper.

"Would you have given that to me if I had said no?" she asked, looking at the paper in my hand.

"This was my ace in the hole," I said with a smile as we started down the road. "After you read that, you would have been running after my car."

She took it and slowly unfolded it. Her eyes slowly moved across the page as my words leapt into her heart. Tears began to well up in her eyes, and she covered her mouth in an open and honest display of emotion that most people dream of feeling just once in their lives.

Pride beamed from inside of me. As Chris had so honestly stated a week ago: "When you write, you try to entice emotion in others." Until tonight, I would have said that was the greatest feeling in the world, but that was before Meagan showed me what it was like to feel unabashedly happy. There might not be such a thing as a perfect world, but there are perfect moments, and these perfect moments are the moments that make life happen. This was my perfect moment.

She finished reading, carefully refolded it, and slid it into her purse. She leaned over and hugged me, placing her soft lips against my neck and repeatedly kissing it as I drove.

"I love it," she whispered, somewhat seductively in my ear.

"That's just for you," I said, shivering slightly from the chill that went down my spine as her voice tickled my ear. "No one else."

"Thank you," she said, kissing me again.

"Are you ready for page one of our adventure, sweetness?" I asked as I pulled on to the main road, heading to somewhere beyond the horizon.